Breaking the Chains

Chloe Harden

Chapter 1

The Evolution

I wouldn't say I'm nostalgic about my past. It's not that. It's more like bound. When I lay back and close my eyes, I can smell the leather, taste the adrenaline, feel the excitement, the thrill of the conquest. Don't get me wrong, I'm glad I'm no longer living the lifestyle, it's just that it seems to have a certain hold over me.

I grew up having to be somewhat of a pleaser. It was how I learned to deal with the trouble of being a kid in my house. There was an endless supply of drinking, yelling, and general abuse doled out by my father, and my mother thought it would be helpful if she criticized pretty much everything about my older sister and myself. I suppose it was her way of coping. We were a "good Christian family", and for them, that meant no matter what hell occurred inside my house, we were always sure to put on a happy face for the rest of the world. In the end, my own way of coping was to learn to be adaptable, always know how to fake it, and, most importantly, trust nobody. I not only took those qualities on, but I wore them like a badge of honour.

Even when I think back to my first boyfriend as a teen, it was nothing more than awkward attempt to be accepted; a feeble effort to make myself think I was good enough. I easily mistook his advances to mean that I held some sort of worth. In the end, the relationships never went far, I learned very little, and I certainly never succeeded in actually becoming close to anyone.

Chapter 2

Meet Dave

I knew I had to hurry; Dave was meeting me at the coffee shop in 15 minutes. I didn't want to fuck this one up. I had distracted myself laying on my bed entertaining thoughts of what it would be like to have Dave bound and gagged and at my mercy. It was an addictive thought pattern, even though I knew it would never, and could never, happen. Dave just wasn't up for that sort of thing. And I liked to think I no longer was either. I noticed I had been caressing myself and allowing my fingertips to linger over my erect nipples and throbbing clit. I was not doing myself any favours showing up to meet him all wet and bothered. I slowly drew up my panties, pulled my shirt back in place, and forced myself out of my reverie and off of the bed.

"Hey, there you are" Dave stood up slowly with a sly grin, as though he could read my thoughts as I strolled into the coffee shop towards him.

"Sorry I was late, I...um...had to...uh..finish something".

Unfortunately, I was a terrible liar, something which I should never attempt. There's just something about Dave. Yes, something alright. He's not like any of the other men I've ever known. It's the kindness in his eyes. The calm feeling I have around him. And there's the undeniable fact that he just simply turns me on. And I can think of nothing better than that rush that courses through my body when I am turned on by a sexy man.

"Come on, let's get out of here," I challenge, while holding eye contact, before I even sit down. Patience has never been a virtue of mine. It's beginning to look like tonight will be no different.

"Please, sit down Cassandra" he directs me. Immediately I sit. He takes my hand between his, focuses his inquisitive brown eyes onto mine, and gives me a smile that melts me immediately. I feel relatively unsettled, not being comfortable succumbing to a man's will, yet unable to stop myself.

"Now let's talk about that book you're working on, how's that going?" Oh right, the book. I had almost forgotten I had shared that with him. In fact, I was starting to regret even having started the book. It had seemed like a good idea at the time, a sort of cathartic release, a way to let go of my past. It was basically chronicling my previous lifestyle, and certainly a lot was coming up for me in the process. In the end, I settled for an iced cap, light conversation about how the book was going, and a whole lot of fantasies (which stayed neatly tucked away in my head unshared).

Chapter 3

The Turning Point

By the time I was 19, I had moved out of my parents' home and was renting a tiny apartment close to downtown. I was working a relatively low-paying, aggressively boring job as a receptionist at an insurance office. My father had arranged this position for me through a friend of his after I graduated high school. I took this as an indication of his lack of confidence in my ability to "adult". At any rate, I spent most of my time working, and when I wasn't working, I was tending to my parents' needs by showing up and looking well put together. My sister had gotten married and moved out the minute she turned 19 and had never looked back, so I was left holding the bag with my parents so to speak. I knew how to say all the right things to show them (and their friends) that I was adulting suitably. I was to be their prize for being pious and loyal to God and family. Around this time, I was beginning to understand the irony. And since I was afraid of entering into another abusive and controlling relationship, but didn't know any alternative, I still tended to hold an impressive distance between myself and men.

That was also the year I made an unlikely new friend. She was an older, more experienced, and very not-boring woman named Alexandria...though she preferred to go by Alex, probably because it made her sound more powerful. Not that Alex needed any help being more powerful. She was the most powerful woman I had ever met, and immediately I was star struck. She was a stark contrast to my own mother, who had always been a shining example of meekness and quiet resignation.

We met at a house party. I had been stuck in the kitchen trying to figure out how to escape the drudgery of a boring conversation when she walked in, grabbed me by the arm and cried "There you are! I've been looking all over for you girl!" and dragged me out of the kitchen with not so much as an apologetic look back at the boring chump we had left in our wake.

"Hi, I'm Alex" she leaned in close and whispered with a giggle as we headed for the living room arm in arm. I could feel her sexuality like a jolt through my system. She wore tight black jeans and a tank top with thigh-high leather boots. Her shiny black hair hung nearly to her waist and she was beautiful in every way. Maybe her eyes were too big, and she certainly had a gap between her front teeth, but somehow these things just made her more beautiful. And she seemed acutely aware of this fact. She appeared to be in her late 20's and never had I ever met anyone more sure of themselves.

Over the next few months, we began to make a habit of hanging out on the weekends. She would invite me for lunch or drinks, and even to some of the parties she attended. One particular Friday night, after a long, boring, and predictable week at work, she had invited me to join her at a house party of a very wealthy older man and a group she mysteriously called "The Executives". She was to pick me up at my house, and she arrived before I had finished getting ready. I poured her a glass of wine, told her I'd be ready shortly, and wandered off to my bedroom to half-heartedly peruse my wardrobe one more time. I was mid-way to putting on my standard blue jeans and t-shirt when I looked up and noticed Alex leaning against my bedroom doorway eying me thoughtfully.

"Hey Cass, why don't you try these?" she suggested as she tossed a pair of tiny black leather shorts my way.

"Oh…." I hesitated, not quite sure if she was being serious or not. They were definitely not the sort of thing I would normally wear, though I had seen her wear something similar before.

"Go on" she smiled encouragingly.

"I don't…I don't know" I mumbled while holding them up skeptically. By the time she was done with me I had the very short very tight leather shorts on, black stiletto heels that she magically produced from her bag, as well as a bright red tank top that seemed scandalous in and of itself.

"There" she declared, standing back to take me in. I was stunned, but somehow allowing her to continue.

"Wait, just one more thing", she reached up and pulled out my neat and tidy ponytail and fluffed out my long blonde locks, which fell to just below my breasts. "Now let's get you into the bathroom to apply a little more eyeliner".

This night was to be the turning point of my life.

Chapter 4

One Night Can Change Everything

When we arrived at the party, I could tell immediately this was not the usual kind of party that Alex took me to. The house was very upscale in one of the nicer neighbourhoods in town. On entering the grand foyer, we were greeted by a well-dressed breathtakingly attractive man who appeared to be in his mid 30's.

"Alex! Come here, I've missed you" he greeted her with a familiar hug and kiss.

"Hi Andre, I'd like to introduce you to Cassandra" she purred suddenly like a coy schoolgirl. She grabbed me by the hand and thrust me toward him.

"Hi....um.... I..." I stammered with my typical awkwardness, "Cass is fine".

"Cassandra" he slowly rolled off his tongue like he was tasting my name. "I prefer Cassandra". Before I could reply he had whisked us through the house, affording me a quick glance past what may have been a study, a library, a drawing room, a living room, a few other rooms I didn't have the chance to document, and finally drawing us out onto the back terrace. What I saw left me curiously horrified, shocked, and exhilarated all at the same time.

I'd like to say that I wasn't totally innocent. Not at all. Well, hardly at all. Well, actually I was, but it's not that I was completely in the dark. I had, after all, attended health class in grade 9. And there was that one boy that I naively called my boyfriend when I was 15. We were together for about six months when I worked at the food court at the mall. We used to meet after work, and he would take me for a drive in his fixed-up Corvette. We would park at the quarry where he would grope me, ram his tongue down my throat, and insist that I stick my hand down his pants. I nearly did. I don't know if it was his bad breath, his bad acne, or his bad manners that stopped me. Anyway, he was 26 and the whole thing was more than creepy. My parents found out, which marked the beginning of even stricter parental supervision, which included driving me to and from work, and monitoring who I hung out with more carefully. My behaviour was not becoming of the nice Christian girl that they claimed to have raised.... and so went the weekly speeches (read beratements) I was now subjected to on my daily rides to and from work. Between their constant supervision, and the terrible example of relationships they offered, I was happy to avoid attempting relationships altogether from that point.

It took me a few moments for my eyes to adjust and focus on what I was seeing. We were standing on a large wooden deck overlooking lavish grounds that included a pool, gardens, and an enormous lawn. There must have been a hundred people sprawled about. Some of them had clothes on. It appeared that I had been brought to some sort of fetish party. I saw women leading men on leashes, men and women wearing nipple clamps and collars, a lot of leather, and a blur of bodies all mingled together and somehow connected to each other. Couples were making out on loungers, one woman was dancing around a pole with an avid audience of both women and men, and there was more than one group participating in what could be deemed "team building" activities. I thought about spinning around and heading for the front door when I felt a hand on my shoulder.

"Cassandra, please.... come". Andre led us down towards the pool area, where someone handed me a blue drink of something dangerously delicious, which I gulped down while staring into my glass wondering, what my parents would say if they could see me now.

After something like the fourth delicious blue drink I began to relax a little. I was perched on a pool-side chair half ignoring the ramblings of a girl who was complaining that her collar was chafing her. I watched as Alex moved about the crowd. She seemed to know most of the people here and she tended to cause a stir everywhere she went.

Eventually the collar-chafed girl wandered off and left me to sit back in my lounger and absorb the atmosphere. As I began to relax, I noticed a shift in myself. I was especially riveted by the women who were barking orders at the men they led around. They seemed so powerful, so sure of themselves. They seemed to be in complete control of the situation. I will admit, I was more than intrigued. I hadn't noticed in the meantime that a man had sat down on the lounger beside mine and was staring intently at me.

"Hello there" He ventured cautiously. I turned to see a very well dressed, slightly older man who had the rugged good looks of an Italian model mixed with a Greek god. And he had an English accent. I was my usual smooth self.

"Hey" I stammered, glancing up at him nervously. I then lost control of my shyness and stared at him with an open-mouthed gape for what felt like 3 hours (probably 30 seconds), wondering what one would say to such an extraordinarily handsome man. I just couldn't bring myself to look away and I had no words, so I just kept staring, heaving my chest up and down in awkward gasps, trying to think of what to say.

"What do you say we get out of here?" he invited; his hungry gaze boring deep into my soul. And then, as if in a dream and led by an unknown force, I took his extended hand and allowed him to lead me away. He took me back into the house and led me through a few corridors. We ended up at a red door, which opened via a push button keypad. Immediately upon entering he grabbed my hands and flung them roughly over my head, pushing me against the back side of the closed door with a small thud. He bit my lip and drove his tongue deep inside my mouth, now clasping both of my wrists in one hand, while dragging the other hand down my face, around my neck, where he paused to briefly grip, and finally resting on my breast. He squeezed gently at first. Then, reaching inside my shirt, aptly freed and aggressively pinched my nipple. My shriek was almost completely stifled by his tongue, which by now was occupying my entire mouth. I had not expected him to pinch so hard.

"That's it. Try to get away" he crooned as I struggled against him.

"I love a fighter!" he went on, completely unaware of my mounting panic.

"How about we use *mercy* as the safe word, ok lover?"

Since I didn't know exactly what that meant I may have made some sort of nodding motion that gave him the encouragement to carry on. What happened next was in parts a blur, and in parts etched forever in my mind.

He began yanking off my skirt with his free hand and shoving his fingers into my pussy roughly. As I screamed out in opposition, he again reminded me how much he loved a fighter. He had dragged me over to the bed and now had me almost completely naked. As he stood to yank down his pants, I managed to break free from him and made a run for the door, which was locked, and apparently required a code to open.

He grabbed me by the hair, now suddenly displeased with my complete lack of obedience, and ordered me back to the bed. When I wouldn't comply, he dragged me back and shoved me face down onto the bed. He held my hips firmly in his strong hands and raised my ass in the air. After briefly licking my ass and my pussy, he began shoving fingers into both repeatedly. In and out, slamming the palm of his hand against my ass, shouting, "Yeah, that's how you like it you little slut, you're going to take it right up the ass you little whore".

I suddenly felt the most excruciating pain as I realized he had shoved his cock inside my ass. I was still screaming and writhing to get away, which fuelled his frenzy to a quick explosive finish not more than 20 seconds after it had begun. He gave my ass one final slap and told me, in an eerily matter of fact voice, to get up and get dressed. I had never felt more ashamed. I felt something die inside me that day.

When I failed to get up and get dressed, he tried, in a more comforting voice, to encourage me to get up. He lifted me slowly off of the bed and turned me around. When he saw the tears staining my cheeks, he grabbed me up close and cooed,

"Baby, I'm sorry, didn't you like it?" He was genuinely confused by this unexpected turn. He stroked my hair and spoke to me like a hurt child.

"Shhh, baby, it's ok, you're fine, you're ok". He handed me my clothes and told me to take my time, he would let Alex know I'd be out in a few minutes. He turned back and looked over his shoulder before leaving the room and shook his head slowly,

"Baby, if I didn't know any better, I would almost swear that was your first time". And with that he exited the door, leaving it unlocked, and leaving me to sit in my shock and horror.

I rolled over in pain and lay staring at the ceiling for a few minutes (or an hour) before slowly getting up and assessing the room. I noticed that the entire room was red and littered with an array of sex toys and other equipment that I couldn't begin to identify. Most likely items designed to inflict pain and/or pleasure. I then noticed a bathroom off to one side of the room. I suddenly raced from the bed and made it to the bathroom in time to wretch uncontrollably into the toilet. I frankly wasn't even concerned with the mess I was making. I moved mechanically into the shower and turned up the hot water. I stood under the water for another few minutes (or an hour) and cleaned myself thoroughly six or seven times before re-emerging hesitantly into the red room. Weirdly, my clothes had been folded neatly and a fresh glass of water was set on the night-stand. I slowly got dressed and reached over to pick up the water, noticing an envelope with my name on it under the glass. With a stomach-wrenching curiosity, I opened the envelope and began to read.

Cassandra, you are exquisite. You deserve every penny of this. I hope we meet again.
Marcus.

Chapter 5

What to Do with Dave

What was I doing with Dave? I often asked myself this question. Dave represented everything I used to say I loathed. Responsibility, maturity, stability. He was a regular grown-up kind of guy. And I....well, what was I really? At 27, I was still trying to figure this out. Did my past define me? Was I defined by my choices moment to moment? Why did I need to define myself at all? If left to my own devices, I could torture myself with this line of questioning endlessly. As I gazed across the coffee shop table at him, I noticed how he listened. I mean really listened. In a way that had me feel heard. I was feeling oddly unsettled by this.

"You were saying?" Dave interrupted my wandering mind.

In my head I was thinking, why are we still sitting at this coffee shop and not back at my place fucking? However, I continued expressing my current frustrations over the character development and plot lines of my book.

Dave and I had had many discussions around what we wanted in a relationship, and in the end, we agreed to hold off on having sex for at least a few months. He claimed it would help us bond emotionally. I was just scared I would fuck up and do something I regretted. We had been together about a month and had been seeing each other several times a week.

We went for dinner, met at coffee shops, took long walks in the city, or simply ran errands together. We had made it a policy not to go to each other's' houses until we were ready to move our relationship into the bedroom.

"So, I was thinking" Dave started one night when we were out for dinner.
"Maybe it's time I cooked you a romantic dinner at my house". I looked up from my plate just in time to catch the mischievous look in his eyes.

Chapter 6

Dinner and a Show

I laboured over what to wear for Dinner at Dave's over the following week. I first chose jeans and a t-shirt, trying not to come across too eager. Then by Tuesday I had decided that sexy lingerie under an overcoat would be perfect. By Wednesday I realized that would be trying too hard. I went somewhere in the middle with a skirt and a blouse with the top few buttons undone. I opted for a new lacy red bra and matching panties that I had felt the need to pick up for the occasion.

When I arrived, Dave was in the kitchen fussing over several dishes that smelled amazing. He greeted me with a warm hug and kiss, poured me a glass of red wine, and ushered me up to the bar stool at the island so I could watch him cook. I was admiring his ripply muscles under his short-sleeved shirt, his flat abs, and, when he turned around, his rock-hard ass. All I kept thinking about was what he would feel like under my hands with his clothes off. I vaguely recall eating steak, salad, some fancy side dish, and drinking more wine. When we were done, I asked if I could help with the dishes, but by then he had other things on his mind.

He took me by the hand and kissed the back of it, then led me off for a "tour of the house". When he opened his bedroom door, I immediately noticed the neatly made bed, plumped up pillows, lit candles, and soft music. I was pretty sure tonight would be the night. I noticed myself breathing quickly in anticipation of what was about to come. This was promising to be a very romantic evening, and I had a pressing urge to have everything about my first "real" relationship to be perfect. He excused himself for a moment and left the room. In that moment the sudden urge came over me to take charge of the situation and I undressed down to my new matching bra and panties.

He breezed back into the room about to hand me my glass of wine, when he stopped short, spilling some of the wine, his mouth dropping open. He immediately put down the wine glasses and came over to me, grasping me about the waist, letting his eyes linger over my body, then looking up into my eyes longingly.

"Oh Cassandra, you take my breath away, you are so beautiful...." he trailed off. I immediately knelt in front of him and undid his pants. As I began sliding them off his hips, I couldn't help but notice his massive erection. I stood up and unbuttoned his shirt and slid it off his shoulders, taking the time to run my hands over his well-built arms and his rippling six pack abs. I was beginning to lose my mind a little. He began murmuring and mumbling incoherently as I knelt back down in front of him and released him from his boxers. He was standing at full attention.... hard and beautiful and all mine. I leaned forward and took him into my mouth.

And then I took him deeper into my mouth. I began running my tongue around the tip of his cock and sucking him in and out while my hand caressed his balls. He began to moan and had my hair in his hands, guiding me to take his cock deeper and deeper. Suddenly he was about to come, and he grabbed my hair with both hands and shoved me onto his cock so hard I couldn't release him, and he shot his hot sticky cum into my mouth with a few last jerks and moans. He suddenly became conscious of what he was doing and began caressing my hair and telling me how amazing that had been. Something in me snapped.

Chapter 7

After the Party

After emerging from the red room, feeling wholly violated, sick to my stomach, and somewhat disoriented, I managed to stumble across Alex and told her we needed to leave immediately. She drove me home in eerie silence. As I reached for the front door, she opened her car window and called out hesitantly,

"Hey Cass". I spun around and looked back at her blankly.

"You did great, I'll see you in a few weeks". She smiled encouragingly, waved and drove off.

I will admit, I cashed the cheque. It was substantial. It paid the month's rent. I realized clearly that I had passed a turning point. One I would have no returning from. And I went anyways. I began to spend a lot of my time and energy avoiding my feelings of shame, guilt, humiliation, and disgust. In order to do so, I had to fill my time with work, shopping, and drinking. I even found myself frequently at the gym racing against time and running from my demons at top speed on the treadmill until I would crumble in exhaustion, head to the shower, and go home to eat dinner and start into a bottle of wine. It was only a matter of time before Alex called again. It happened two weeks later.

"Hey Cass" she began cheerfully, but with a slight note of hesitation in her voice.

"So, there's this party...." This time I didn't argue when she showed up at my door, tossed me a bag of clothes, and stated flatly,

"Wear these". She left me alone to dress while she moved about my kitchen helping herself to a glass of wine. I took my time holding up the items one by one. First out of the bag was a pair of thigh-high lacy stay-ups. Next out of the bag was a mini.... skirt? I assumed this was a skirt, however it did not promise to fully cover my ass. This was followed by a bustier that laced up in the front. I managed to get all laced up, covered up, and pulled up. I had some comfort in knowing the panties I had pulled from my drawer were full coverage, but still classy and sexy. And of course, there was no need for a bra. I put back on the spiked heels from last time, applied fresh red lipstick, and gave my voluminous hair a shake. I emerged from my bedroom and, judging by Alex's reaction, I believe I may have looked super hot.

"Holy shit" she started.

"You look fucking hot". And there was something new in her eyes I couldn't put my finger on, but she definitely looked pleased. As I shut the front door behind me, I spun around looking for her car, and was more than a little surprised to find a limo parked in front of the building. The driver quickly emerged from the car, bustled around to the back door, opened it with a flourish and announced "ladies", waving us in. Once inside, I began to giggle. I had never been in a limo and was surprised by how roomy and lavish it was. Alex immediately poured us each a drink and, holding her glass up, cheered to us and our adventures to come. As it turned out, the limo ride was going to be over an hour long, so we were going to have plenty of time to drink.

As we sat facing each other laughing and drinking, Alex suddenly looked me in the eyes and calmly said,

"Uncross your legs". Without breaking eye contact I uncrossed my legs. Then she coolly suggested I spread my legs. Again, without breaking eye contact, I spread my legs. She then shifted her eyes hungrily towards my pussy. She quickly looked up at me, eyebrows raised and burst out in clear disapproval,

"Cass take those off. Do it now". When I met her gaze, I saw that look again. This time I understood. I wanted to know what she would do, so I retaliated with "Why don't you take them off if you want them off so badly". The next thing I knew she had knelt down in front of me and was sliding my very short skirt up until she could get a hold of the top of my panties with her fingertips. I lifted my hips from the seat in sudden anticipation, and then she paused and looked up at me. She then reconsidered, and instead of pulling down my panties she grazed her hand lightly over them, brushing me gently and stirring up a surprising amount of arousal. With her thumb she gently began rubbing over my mound, sliding up and down and beginning to drive me wild. Then she slowly, gently slid her finger under my panties sideways, caressing me lightly with the back of her finger, barely grazing my clit and causing me to arch towards her hand as I let out a small moan. I leaned back and closed my eyes and decided to just relax and take it all in. I felt her pull my panties aside and when I looked down, she was eying up my pussy lustfully.

"Cass, I want to taste you so badly, I want to eat your pussy" she licked her lips thoughtfully and met my eyes. I was so turned on in a way I had never been before. With a small moan I begged her to please taste me and pushed my pussy up towards her awaiting mouth.

"Patience" she scolded. She began by leaning in close and I could feel her breath on me. She was breathing me in and telling me how great I was going to taste. I stole a glance down at her and, as she looked up at me, she held out her tongue softly and slowly licked me from back to front without spreading my lips. She did this again and again and had me panting and begging for more.

"That's right, beg me, tell me what you want, tell me I can do anything I want to you. Tell me you belong to me".

"Yes, yes, please, I beg you, I am all yours, please fuck me with your tongue Alex, I want you to suck my clit, fuck my cunt with your tongue!" I pleaded in desperation. I began gasping and coming closer to climax. She suddenly parted my pussy lips and lunged her tongue deep inside me while continuing to work my clit with her thumb. Just when I was about to come, she stopped and ordered me to turn over. I used the length of the limo seat to perch on my hands and knees and she positioned herself behind me. She pulled off my panties and threw them on the floor. I felt her spreading my ass cheeks apart, and then I experienced the most exquisite feeling as she slid her tongue across my ass, poking and probing at my hole, meanwhile she re-inserted her thumb into my pussy and started ramming me harder and harder, playing with my clit with her fingers, reaching up and yanking my breast out of the bustier and twisting and pinching my nipple. It was all too much and suddenly I started spasming and coming and twisting and felt my whole body wracked with one orgasm after another until I collapsed face down onto the seat, panting and gasping.

Eventually I rolled over and laid on my side comfortably, looking across the limo at her. She was neatly sitting, legs crossed, sipping her wine, looking smug.

"I see you like women" was her first comment. Well, to be honest, I had no idea that I liked women until now.

"Next time, you'll see to me" she proclaimed.

The party we went to that night was full of businessmen in suits, women in dangerously skimpy outfits, and free flowing booze and coke. I declined the coke, obviously.... I wasn't stupid. This time I knew what was expected of me. When a pasty middle aged half-drunk man with a wedding ring tan line approached me, asking if I'd like to go "play", I saucily replied, "There's nothing I would like more". The event was substantially unremarkable. He put his doughy white dick into me, I spit on my hand and rubbed it on my pussy when he wasn't looking and proceeded to tell him how hot he was making me and how much I wanted him to fuck me hard. While the sad little man fucked my pussy and I murmured words I thought sounded sexy, I thought about how much I might earn for this, and what I might go shopping for later that week.

Chapter 8

The Aftermath with Dave

Dave and I never ended up having sex that night. After he held my head and came down my throat I full-on panicked, grabbed my stuff, ran off to the bathroom to throw on my clothes, and hightailed it out of his apartment without so much as a backwards glance. I tortured him for the rest of the week by refusing his calls, ignoring his texts, and avoiding our usual hangouts. While I was busy ignoring him, I had some time to think. I began with a good healthy dose of wrong making, followed by some good old-fashioned guilt, and then threw in some shame to round out my week. By Friday evening I was a mess, as was my relationship, neither of which I knew how to fix. So, I called Alex. Luckily, with everything we had been through, we had somehow managed to maintain our friendship, and she was the one person I knew I could turn to.

"Alex, I fucked up" I began. Luckily for me, she cleared her schedule and told me when and where to meet her for a drink.

"So, you're still struggling to find your way I see..." and we continued to talk into the night, me letting it all out while she nodded, listened, and offered her advice here and there. By the end of the night, I was feeling much more capable of going back in and trying again with Dave. I was pretty confident I just needed to apologize and explain a few things to him, and we would get right back on track.

I called Dave the next morning, and, since it was Saturday, figured we could spend the day together to get things sorted. Dave did not pick up. Maybe he was sleeping in. I tried texting him. After waiting an hour and getting no reply I began to panic. I did what I never should have done, and I got in my car and drove over to his place. I knocked on his front door, wondering why he hadn't responded to my texts and phone calls, since his car was parked out front. He eventually answered the door. He was wearing boxers. I assumed he had been sleeping. He had not been sleeping. This became imminently obvious when a busty redhead walked out of the bedroom wearing Dave's robe and asked Dave if everything was ok. My world crashed down around me and once again I found myself running.

While frantically fumbling to get my car door open, I could hear Dave call out half-heartedly to me, but I did not stick around to see what he was going to say, I flung open the door, heaved myself into the driver's seat, and squealed off down the street, heart racing, head pounding, not sure where I was going. About 6 blocks away I pulled over and burst into a heaving sobbing mess. I must have sat there in my car crying for 15 minutes at least before my breathing slowed down and I began to dry my eyes and assess the situation. It appeared Dave had given up on me and moved on (very quickly too I thought as a gut-wrenching pain shot through my stomach). I suddenly felt a wave of nausea come over me, and wrenched open my car door, falling out just in time to throw up all over a nicely manicured lawn. When I looked up and wiped my mouth an elderly man was sitting on his porch watching me. Exhausted and humiliated, I climbed back into my car and drove home.

Chapter 9

Sliding Deeper

A few weeks after the doughy white fuck, sitting on a patio enjoying a liquid lunch with Alex, she asked me how I felt about the parties we had been going to. This was her way of asking if I was ok with the fact that I had begun having sex for money. We engaged in a lengthy chat about it, and I somehow realized that I was actually ok with this. That is, as long as I didn't have a repeat of the first night. That was definitely not my style. However, it seemed as though my self-esteem did not require me to not be a prostitute to feel ok about myself, or, more likely, I actually had no self-esteem to protect. I'm pretty sure I had very little clarity on any of it at the time. I just knew that I didn't want to feel taken advantage of, and somehow taking the money gave me a sense of power and control. I agreed to a number of more unremarkable parties over the following months and all of the occasions were relatively alike. I had unremarkable sex with some less-than mediocre men and made an exceptionally large amount of money. And I don't mean the kind of money the street walking girls make. These men paid extremely well for my services. Around this time, I also started making a habit of showing up late for my job at the insurance office, and often called in sick. I had just become such drudgery to work so hard for such little pay.

After about six months of raking in undue amounts of money I noticed that the feelings of power and control I had been gaining by taking their money was starting to wane. Alex began encouraging me to wear a slightly different style of clothing to the parties, and she began directing me away from certain men and towards others. One evening when I was dressed in a leather mini skirt, thigh-high boots, and leather straps across my chest Alex asked me if I was interested in trying something new. A lot of men had been asking for me that night, but Alex kept directing me away from them with a series of unconvincing excuses. I asked what she meant, and she led me away to a back room in the house, where 5 or 6 people were scattered on couches messing with something on the glass table. They looked up when we walked in - almost with an air of paranoia - until Alex told them to relax, we were there to join them. They made room for us on the sofa, so we squeezed in between a greasy looking man who was talking too fast and an anxious looking young woman who kept fiddling with her hair. The man was bent over the table arranging a white powder into a line, which I assumed was coke, and then he bent farther over, snorted a few lines up a straw, and then leaned back and closed his eyes. The woman then picked up the straw with shaking hands, leaned over the table, and snorted two lines up her nose quickly. She also leaned back and suddenly relaxed, closed her eyes, and began to smile. Alex told me to watch her as she grabbed the straw, leaned over a line, and sniffed it up her left nostril, leaned over another line and sniffed it up her right nostril. She then passed me the straw.

What happened next seemed like the most natural thing in the world. The other two had already left, romping out of the room holding hands and laughing wildly. After I snorted the coke, I realized that everything was actually perfect in my previously shitty life and I knew that I could, in fact conquer the world should I chose to. Alex took me back to the party, and I was super pumped to get the party rolling. She walked straight up to two handsome businessmen in suits, pulled them aside, and had a short conversation with them while I grabbed a drink, danced provocatively through the dimly lit base-thumping room, and let someone grind up against me from behind to the beat of the music. Alex grabbed me on the way out of the room with the two men in tow and told me to follow her lead. Since I was up for pretty much anything, I tossed my head back, laughed out loud, and let her lead me away.

When we got into the room, Alex turned on some red and black lights and ordered the men to get down on their knees. She assigned one of them to me and she took control of the other. She handed me a leash, which made me laugh, and told me to take my job more seriously. I was instructed to take charge of my man, so I fastened his collar around his neck and told him to be a good boy. Alex led her man out of the room and left us to work it out.

At first, I giggled as I tugged on his leash and pulled him around the room. He never smiled or spoke, except to say yes ma'am, thank you ma'am, and yes please. I told him to sit, stay, lay down, roll over, and treated him like a dog in every way I could think of. And he was completely ok, or even more than ok, with all of it.

I was having a good chuckle though I noticed I was starting to feel a warm sensation creeping up my stomach and down my thighs. I wanted to test my limits and his, so I straightened up my face and spoke a little firmer. I looked down at him and he was still looking up at me with devotion and obedience. I was starting to really warm up to this. I tried scolding him and he immediately apologized. Then something in me released and I really started to let him have it.

"Stop staring at me, you're nothing but a low life dog, you don't even deserve to look at me!". He immediately looked down at the floor and corrected his behaviour. I ordered him to sit on his haunches looking at the floor, which he immediately did. I put down his leash and wandered over to the rack of equipment and perused the various options. I settled on an imposing piece with a wooden handle and long draping leather straps. I was pretty sure this was an ideal place to start.

For some reason, I broke free that night. I unleashed a whipping on him that liberated me. I whipped him for every man I took money from after having sex, I whipped him for what Marcus did to me, and I whipped him to make up for all the loss of power I had ever felt. I was punishing him. And the amazing part was that he was loving it. He begged for more and I gave him more. In the end I crumpled on the floor exhausted and spent, resting my head on my bent knees. I was afraid to look up. I may have sat like that for 15 minutes before I dared to glance up at him. He was sitting staring at me awaiting further instruction. His shoulders and back looked welted and sore. I looked away.

"You can, uh, go" I swallowed without looking back at him. He thanked me and quietly got up and moved about for a moment before exiting the room. I laid back and stretched out on the floor. My muscles were actually aching from the workout I had just had. I had clearly come down from my coke high and was beginning to feel sleepy. The next thing I knew Alex was leaning over me,

"Cass, Cass, wake up, it's time to go".

Chapter 10

A Pleasant Surprise on My Way Down

T he next day I woke up, poured myself a coffee, and went about my usual Sunday business. I laid on the living room floor staring up at the ceiling, had another cup of coffee, brushed my hair, laid back down, changed into even more comfortable pyjamas, read the flyers on my counter, checked my emails, and stared out the window for a while. It had been a while since I had bothered to show up for work, and I was pretty sure I was fired anyways. I thought it might be a good idea to make it official, since I certainly did not need the insignificant cheques that I was receiving from my day job anyhow. I decided that on Monday I would call in and tell them I had been very much under the weather and was going to move away and anyhow would be quitting effective immediately. I am pretty sure I forgot to make that phone call.

Things spiralled downhill from there. I mostly only needed to work on Saturday nights with Alex, which had me making more cash than I knew what to do with. So, I stepped up my drinking and took up smoking. Some days I would shop for expensive clothes and shoes, some days I would forget to shower, and just sit in a cafe or pub sipping drinks and smoking, watching strangers walk by.

I began to get bored and lonely. I was sitting at a coffee shop one Tuesday afternoon, when a lovely young woman with long chestnut hair, big eyes, and sloppy clothes walked in slinging a tote bag over her shoulder and looking like she had misplaced something. She dropped all of her stuff in the middle of the shop and began rummaging through her bag looking perplexed and annoyed.

"Dammit" she muttered to herself while re-checking her pockets and dumping out her bag onto the floor. She was clearly spiralling in agitation. I thought the whole thing was quite entertaining, so I giggled a little and clapped my hand over my mouth. Her head jerked up and she stared me down.

"What exactly is so funny over there? Am I amusing you?"

"Well," I began. "Yeah, you kind of are actually". "Looks like you misplaced something..."

"Well shit yeah, I can't find my money. I had a $20 when I left my place this morning to walk the dogs. There were four of them today and they got me kind of tangled up. I must have dropped it somewhere on the street." She looked like she might have started to tear up if I hadn't jumped in.

"I'll buy, what are you having...it's on me today...just think of it as your lucky day" and I winked at her and approached the counter to pay for her coffee and insisted on buying her a sandwich as well. She didn't look like she ate often enough.

"Thanks" she muttered between bites, her eyes shining up at me, a grin spreading across her face.

"By the way, I'm Annalisa. But you can call me Lili". Lili was possibly the weirdest girl I had ever met. I liked her instantly. As it turns out, her story was one of abuse and neglect by a drugged-out mother who was usually stoned, and her come-and-go scumbag boyfriends; many of whom took their liberties with Lili as they pleased throughout her childhood. She seemed unfazed by most of what she told me, but I noticed she seemed a bit twitchy when she talked about the boyfriends. I suspect she hadn't come to the point of realizing what a shitty life she had had, and acted a bit spaced out and chill to avoid thinking about it.

In less than a week I had invited Lili to live with me. She accepted immediately. We settled into a very nice domestic arrangement. She walked dogs every morning, I sat on the patio and smoked. We cooked breakfast together, and then went for a walk to do something unexpected, weird, or unexplainable. One day we went bed shopping for no reason and climbed under the covers, pretending to sleep until the sales lady crisply asked us to leave. Another time we dressed up like witches and pretended to cast spells at people from a park bench. One day, after watching the Sound of Music, we went to a thrift shop and dressed ourselves up like the characters from the movie and danced around town singing our favourite songs from the movie. We laughed a lot that day, finally falling onto each other in hysterics at the park where she walked the dogs. As we lay tangled, she looked down at me, staring straight into my eyes and declared

"Cass, I love you, you're the best friend I ever had!" I knew at that moment I would do anything for this girl.

Chapter 11

The Anxiety

I got back to my house after seeing Dave with that red-headed slut (of course, what else could she be?), and ended up pacing around my apartment wondering what to do to ward off the anxiety. I could feel my stomach still in knots, my breath still tasted of puke, and, when I caught a glimpse of myself in the mirror, I was a little shocked at how disheveled and wild-eyed I looked. I sat down, stood up, paced some more, wandered over to my fridge, opened it, closed it, and wandered down the hall to the bathroom. I contemplated taking a shower, but that seemed impossibly taxing. I sat back down on the couch and started drumming my fingers against the arm rest. I recognized that I was starting to have a full anxiety attack. I began to feel light-headed; I noticed my breathing became more rapid, and I began rocking back and forth with my head in my hands.

"Ahhhhgh" gurgled out of my throat and I threw my head against the back of the couch staring up at the ceiling. I grabbed my head and began pulling at my hair from both sides and then grabbed a pillow and shoved the corner of it into my mouth to stifle a scream. I tried to get up from the couch, and suddenly the tears began again. This time I slumped to the floor, curled up, holding my knees, and sobbed uncontrollably. I rocked and cried like that for 15 or 1000 minutes, and then rolled onto my back and stared up at the ceiling again, sniffling and winding down to a dull whimper.

I had hit rock bottom before. This felt familiar. Only I knew better this time. I actually had my shit together now. I was working at a job I loved, was completely off drugs and alcohol, had quit smoking, was working on writing a book, and had been (had been) dating a very nice man.

I forced myself up and dried my tears roughly. I heard a voice in the back of my head telling me not to, but I grabbed my coat and headed out to the street anyways. I launched myself down the street with a certain intention and stopped at the door of an Irish pub that had cheap drinks between 4 and 6 pm. It was 4:15 pm. At around 7 pm I have a sketchy recollection of stumbling out of the pub recklessly with a shaggy looking middle-aged man who was nearly as drunk as I was. We laughed and stumbled up the street, swaying and lurching across the sidewalk until we reached my apartment. I managed to buzz us in after trying 4 or 5 times, which just made us laugh harder. I stopped to puke on the lobby floor a little, laughed, may have said "oops" and headed for the elevator with my shaggy date in tow. When we got inside, I immediately poured us two glasses of wine, which we chugged, and then he immediately lunged on top of me, his wet sloppy tongue pressing into my mouth. I had a certain amount of awareness of finding him revolting but was in a frenzy to fuck Dave out of my mind. We fumbled awkwardly out of our pants, attempted to kiss again, and then decided to get straight to it. I was far from turned on, so I found myself spitting on my hand and quickly rubbing myself to accommodate his half flaccid cock. I tried stroking him for a few minutes, and then just let him start shoving into me. He lasted around 5 minutes, during which time I put up a good show of moaning and grabbing his ass, cooing,

"Yeah baby, ram that cock into me, I love it, harder baby, that's it". He shot his cum into me, rolled off, laid there for a few minutes, and then excused himself and went to the bathroom.

"Hey baby, that was great, thanks", he called from the bathroom.

He came back in, still naked, and flicked a towel at me.

"We'll have to do that again some time". And with that, he grabbed his clothes, stumbled to yank them on, and slammed the door shut on his way out.

Chapter 12

Crawling Back to Sanity

I woke up the Sunday morning with a vague recollection of having made a terrible choice the night before. I had about 30 seconds of undeserved ignorance before it all came back to me in one terrifying jolt through my gut. I rolled out of bed, stumbled to the bathroom, and managed to do most of the violent puking into the toilet. The retching eventually stopped. A new low had been reached for sure. I questioned the validity of my existence in that moment, as I slumped over the toilet with my forehead resting on the seat. That was the moment I heard a knock on my door. A knock on my door? I lived in an apartment building, people didn't just knock on my door, they had to be buzzed in. For some reason I was compelled to stand up, take a swipe across my face as though that would clean the puke off, and grabbed a robe on the way to the door. I opened it, more out of curiosity than good sense, still under a very hung-over fog.

What I hadn't expected was to see Dave standing there. I would have been less surprised to see the queen of England or my dead grandmother. I had no words. I stood there half covered by an old robe, puke smeared on my face, with last night's make-up smudged under my eyes looking more like a crack whore caught in a back alley than a respectable woman in her late 20's with a good job and a decent life. I stared at Dave. Dave stared back at me. I opened my mouth to speak, but nothing came out. He cocked his head to one side, opened his mouth, then closed it again, squinting his eyes as though it would make me come into better focus, thereby explaining what he was looking at. Then a twinkle showed up in his eyes and the corners of his mouth began to twitch. I looked up at him, prepared to die of mortification, and instead, caught the look on his face, and suddenly we both began to giggle. The giggles turned into outright laughter, then I hiccupped loudly, and the neighbour opened his door, told us to shut it or move it, and then slammed his door in an indignant huff. I forgot that I resembled a crack whore for a moment, and we stood together at my door having a good side-clutching laugh. Dave wound down first, and then a look of concern came over his face.

"I'm worried about you Cass."

"I'm fine, don't worry about me", I attempted to lie to him. He ignored my feeble attempt to hide my distress.

"Come on, let's get you inside and sort this out" he ordered, and led me back inside like a petulant child.

He directed me to the bathroom, spun me around, removed my robe, and pushed me towards the shower. I heard him breathe in sharply and breathe out an almost audible moan as he watched me move away from him naked and into the shower. I was pretty shocked that in my disheveled state he still found me desirable. I showered the night off of me as though I could wash it down the drain. Dave wandered back into the bathroom to see if I was ok. I responded by shutting off the water and stepped out into the embrace of a fluffy towel hug. He wrapped the towel around me, tucked it in, and told me to meet him in the living room after my teeth were brushed. I wanted to take offence, but he had an excellent point. Besides, he had cleaned up my puke. He had cleaned up my puke. I tried to let that sink in.

I timidly opened the bathroom door and saw him sitting on the couch, head back, eyes closed. I tip-toed over to him, staring down at him.

"Why are you staring at me Cass?" he asked in a half-mocking tone without opening his eyes. He then opened his eyes, squinting at me again, and grabbed my hand to pull me down to the couch beside him.

Chapter 13

The Re-Construction

Dave and I ended up talking for hours. He told me that he had made a terrible mistake inviting that girl back to his house after meeting her the night before at a bar. He admitted that in his hurt and rejection, he'd had a one-night stand with her to try to force me out of his mind, and that it made him feel sick when he thought about it. When he finished retelling the story of his Friday night, he paused, looked over at me, and asked if I was ok. I vaguely nodded, feeling a little sick inside. The thought of him sleeping with another woman made me feel like I had been punched in the stomach. I wanted to throw up all over again, but there was nothing left. He sat back and eyed me up thoughtfully before asking me if I was ready to tell him what had happened on my Saturday night. I nodded solemnly and began my story.

"After I left your house, I thought I would die of sadness, anger, remorse, and humiliation. It turns out none of those things killed me, so out I set out on a reckless tear and ended up taking a man home that I met at the bar and trying to fuck you out of my head. It didn't work. All I ended up with is a very bad head-ache, a lot of nausea, and a whole bunch of guilt and regret."

Dave wrapped his arms around me and whispered into my hair that he loved me. I mumbled back into his shirt that I loved him too. I lifted my head to meet his eyes and that's when I saw that he was looking at me with complete love. It rocked me to the core, and in that moment, I swore to myself I would never again do anything to jeopardize what we had.

He lifted me off the couch and carried me into my bedroom. He laid me on the bed and crawled up beside me. He stared down at me again with so much love in his eyes that I teared up before wrapping my arms around his neck and drawing him close enough to kiss. His warm soft lips were like salvation. I kissed him as though consuming him was the only thing standing between me and total starvation. Finally, he pulled away, gently removing my arms from around his neck, and told me he thought it was best if he left. I understand now that he did not want our first time to be like this.

Chapter 14

Lili's Entry

Lili had been living with me for about 4 months when Alex started to take an interest in her. Generally speaking, Lili dressed in bohemian style clothes and acted a little spaced out. I didn't mind that she didn't contribute to the rent or bills. She would usually end up giving most of her dog-walking money to homeless people or would come home with food from the market and cook us supper. She did her share of the domestic duties, and, more than anything, she kept me company. One night when Alex stopped by to brief me on an upcoming party, I saw her looking over at Lili with her head cocked to the side. I knew that look; I had seen it before. When Lili left the room, Alex turned to me and asked,

"So, what's that girl's deal anyways?" I explained that she was a bit of a free spirit, had had a tough life, and was one of the sweetest, most generous people I knew. She could tell that I was beginning to feel defensive and protective of her. But Alex pressed on, "So what does she do for money?"

When Lili came back into the room, I didn't even have time to step in, or warn Lili what was coming. Alex moved across the room and sat down beside Lili on the couch. She began to speak in a calm soothing tone. "It's Lili, right? What an interesting name. You know, I've never really sat down to get to know you. I think it's time you and I became friends!" Alex asked Lili a lot of questions, gave her a lot of compliments, and beamed at her as she listened as though completely absorbed in everything Lili said. Eventually Lili began to open up and soon they were discussing men, relationships, Lili's childhood, and what her life aspirations were. Alex asked if I had any wine, and soon a few bottles had been uncorked and consumed. Alex was good. By the end of the second bottle the two were carrying on like best friends, and all I could do was sit there watching it like a train wreck in slow motion. I witnessed most of the conversation, other than a few times I had to leave the room for something, and I figured I could do any required damage control later. After Alex finally left at around 2 in the morning, Lili immediately turned to me, narrowed her eyes, and with an accusing look demanded to know why I had been excluding her from all the fun that I had been having with Alex. Oh shit.

I spent the next several days trying to explain that I hadn't been excluding her, I just really didn't think that this lifestyle was for her. "Well Alex thinks I'd be really good at it" she would argue back endlessly. I was getting tired of hearing "Alex thinks this" and "Alex thinks that". They had begun to talk on the phone almost every night - I would hear her giggling and half-heartedly arguing with Alex "No, I'm not, you're way prettier" and "Oh, I would never be as good at that as you are!" I could easily see how Alex was grooming her. Had she groomed me the same way? I began to wonder about that, but put it out of my mind, as thinking about it was beginning to make me feel agitated.

The following Friday afternoon Lili advised me that Alex was coming over to give her a make-over. Double shit. She arrived with a few bottles of wine and a bag of goodies. Out came the short shorts, miniskirts, skimpy tops, and the high heels. "Ooh" and "Aah" went Lili, and Alex beamed through the whole thing. By the end of two bottles of wine (while I stood by watching and drinking until this seemed ok), Lili was wearing a black tube top, a glittery mini skirt, and silver stilettos. Alex showed her how to curl her hair into voluptuous waves with a large rod curling iron and left her with some make-up tips and demonstrations. Alex had promised Lili that if she did well with the make-over she would bring her to our Saturday night event.

Chapter 15

Lili is Broken

By Saturday afternoon Lili was buzzing. "Oh Cass, it's going to be so much fun tonight!" She went on like an overenthusiastic schoolgirl going on her first date. She was told she would just be coming to hang out, look pretty, and have fun, but that there would be no expectations of her tonight. By the time Alex arrived Lili had on full hair and makeup and swooped over to the door in her stiletto heels to greet Alex at the door with a flourish. "Alex, I'm soooo excited about tonight" she began with a dramatic flair. "Stand back, let me take a look at you" insisted Alex while holding Lili at arm's length. There was a long pause while Alex stared her up and down, eventually asking her to spin, bend over, walk, twirl. Lili did as she was told like an obedient child, looking up earnestly into Alex's face, hoping desperately for the approval she was seeking. Finally, Alex broke into a warm smile, eyes twinkling, and pulled Lili close for a hug. "Lili, you look absolutely amazing. I would do you!" Something wrenched a little in my gut when she said that, but luckily, I was quickly able to drink it away with a swift chug of my wine. I did one final check in the mirror to confirm I still looked hot (even though I was feeling a little bit invisible). I did my best to look completely unfazed, and we headed out the door.

The party was of the usual sort. There was an assortment of men in suits breezing about having important conversations with each other, smartly dressed women on some of their arms, and some groups of women standing together chatting. And then there were the "party girls". We were easy to identify. We all had on stilettos, very short skirts or shorts. Some, most, or nearly all of our generously ample chests were on display, and all of us appeared to be in our early 20's and were all very beautiful. I recognized some of the other girls from various parties I had been to over the past year, and there were some new faces that looked barely legal. A small part of me felt a bit sad, or even protective of these girls. A few appeared as nervous as Lili, and I guessed it was their first time as well. I tried to keep Lili close, sort of watch over her, but a gentleman glided up behind me, pressing his hand against my lower back, curling it around the front, and whispered into my ear that he heard I have some very special talents. The next hour was spent in a secluded room servicing his need to be flogged, humiliated, ordered about, and generally dominated. He was one of the few that actually wanted sex, however not the usual kind. He begged me to fuck his ass with a strap-on while continuing to flog him, pull on his nipple clamps, and degrade him. I gave him an extra treat of ramming inside his ass with very little warning or preparation. I could tell I was hurting him, his screams were not just in ecstasy, but a very chilling combination of ecstasy and agony. The very point I had honed my skills at holding men at. I knew how to push them to the very brink of how much pain they could take before passing out, and how to layer and build sexual pressure higher and higher before finally letting them have their big release just prior to passing out. Most of my clients would kill or die for this experience. This is why I usually walked out of a Saturday night with one to two thousand dollars in my pocket. Tonight was promising to be a profitable night. I left my "date" in the room to collect himself at his own pace and found a place to clean up and prepare to re-enter the party. I knew he would find me later to produce an envelope full of cash.

As I walked back towards the main party, I found myself wondering what sort of night Lili was having. I knew she was putting on a very brave and enthusiastic face but had to have been nervous inside. I assumed I would maybe find her chatting with the other party girls, or quietly chatting up a gentleman or two. I looked around and didn't see her, so I moved to another party room where they were playing music and starting to couple up. It took my eyes a few minutes to adjust before I spotted her. I was stunned. She was up on a coffee table gyrating to the music, running her hands over herself, and appeared to be entertaining at least four men who stood leering and encouraging her. A few of them were running their hands over her, and one of them pulled her tube top down and started fondling and sucking on her breasts. She threw her head back and moaned and looked like she was completely lost in the moment. I watched in horror as one of the others began running his hands up her thighs, pushing her skirt up over her ass. A few others joined in and were rubbing her ass, her tits, and even her pussy. One stepped in front of her, bent over, and dove right into her pussy with his mouth. He was bobbing his head up and down, licking her and probing her, and she appeared to be loving every minute of it. The rest of the room either watched with delight or ignored them for their own fun. A few more men joined in, and many of them started grabbing their dicks out of their pants and began stroking themselves while watching, touching, or licking her. She was still up on the table, and I was still standing across the room watching, frozen to my spot. I knew I couldn't do anything, it would be a party foul for me to step in, so I just kept watching while one of the men scooped her up and carried her out of the room, while several men followed, cheering and looking dangerously aggressive. I worried about her but didn't know where they had gone. I tried to distract myself with wandering about. I found Alex and asked if she knew where Lili was, but she waved me off and said she was sure she was having a good time. I wandered around the mansion to see if I could find her. A few minutes later I heard cheering and moaning and screaming coming from one of the rooms. I tried the door, but it was locked. I quickly went back to find Alex and shouted at her "Lili is in trouble, get me into that fucking room!". Alex walked away. I rushed back to the room to find it quiet. I gently opened the door and was sick to my stomach at what I saw.

Lili was lying in a heap on the floor, naked, covered in cum, blood, and her own tears. She was whimpering and calling my name. I rushed to her side and looked down at her, telling her I was here, it was ok now. I managed to get her up to the adjoining bathroom and put her in the shower. I was having a hard time rounding up her clothes, but I found a simple cotton dress in the closet and put that on her. I sat her on the bed, pushed back her hair, and wiped the smeared makeup off her cheeks. She was still staring straight ahead as though in a state of shock. I didn't want to ask her any questions tonight, I just needed to get her home. I took her by the hand and led her out past the party. I couldn't find Alex, but I didn't care, I just wanted to get in a cab and go. As we passed the main party room my gentleman date rushed up and pressed an envelope into my hand, thanking me for a very extraordinary evening, and as we were walking out of the room someone called to Lili. She stopped, turned around, and made eye contact with one of her abusers. He rushed over to her, kissed her on the cheek, and pressed an envelope against her chest. When he released it, it fell to the floor. Lili kept walking. I stooped over to pick it up, tucked it into my purse, and followed her out the door to the waiting cab.

Once home, I tucked her into bed and retired to my own room before remembering the envelopes. I checked mine - $2000. Wow, he really was impressed. These were the sort of men who did not need to be given a price in advance. They knew they would not be invited back to these parties if they were known as cheap or lacking gratitude. I reached back in and pulled out Lili's envelope. I was stunned when I counted $4000. I assumed each of the four men had contributed $1000. I put in on my nightstand and went to sleep.

The next morning when I woke up the house was still quiet. I put on a pot of coffee and sat on the porch waiting for Lili to wake up. About an hour later the sliding door began to open very slowly. Lili looked like hell. Her hair was wild, her makeup was smudged, and she was wearing only a tank top and panties, as though fully dressing was too much effort. She sat down on the seat beside me, staring at the view of the city, not looking at me. "They used me Cass" was all she said. "They hurt me."

After a while a looked sideways at her. I could see her wheels turning, and eventually asked her what was going on inside her mind. She turned and looked at me and said "You know, they used me, and I deserved it. I have been broken for a long time, and last night they finally shattered me". She began to tell me the tale of the night. After I left, she wasn't sure what to do with herself, and a couple of party girls invited her to go to a back room with them, which is where they coaxed her into trying coke, telling her it would loosen her up and make her feel on top of the world. This was just prior to her getting up on the table to dance. She told me that the four main men took turns raping her once they got her to the bedroom. In the front, in the back, sometimes both at once. All this while other men stood over watching and stroking themselves until they came on her chest, face, anywhere they wanted. She didn't really consider it rape, though she also didn't consider it consensual. She was pretty messed up. She asked me if I thought she deserved what she got. I was in the middle of protesting when I remembered the envelope. I excused myself and ran to get it from my bedroom. I came back out on the deck and dropped it in her lap. She looked up confused "what is this?" but I just nodded at it and told her to open it.

As she pulled out the $4000, she looked confused. "What will I do with all this money Cass?" she looked like such a child as she asked.

"Well, for starters, you could try spending it on yourself for once". She said she wasn't comfortable with that, so we settled on keeping half, and giving half away. We decided to get up and go hit the town and see what we could do with a pocket full of cash.

Chapter 16

A Pocket Full of Cash

Lili and I stopped at the grocery store and stocked up, and then she led me to some of her favourite haunts. First, we went to an abandoned warehouse and climbed up some back steps, over a few sleeping people, and down a dark musty hallway. We entered a large space with no glass in the windows to protect from the elements. There were several people lurking, sleeping, shooting up, or sitting and rocking. A few people looked up suspiciously when we entered, and Lili quickly let them know we were friends and had come to help. She reached into her over-stuffed bag and pulled out some sandwiches, snacks, drinks, and cash. She gave each person some of each, wished them well, and off we went to a back alley where a few more of her acquaintances resided and dispersed more of the goods and cash. After we hit a few more of her favourite spots, we began to cruise the streets for homeless people, especially the kids, and we made a few more stops at food marts along the way to replenish the stocks. By the end of about 8 hours of walking, talking with people, handing out food and money and having an overall amazing day, we went back home, drained and happy. "That was the best day of my life Cass, I feel like some kind of angel" gushed Lili before grabbing a beer, cracking it open, and retiring to her bedroom for the night.

Monday morning Lili came out of her room and announced that she needed a new wardrobe if she was going to continue her new venture as The Street Angel. After a quick breakfast we went to one of the fancier shopping malls and we blew the $2000 on shoes, coats, purses, skirts, tops, lingerie, and makeup. It was so much fun helping her shop that I almost forgot why we were shopping for all of this. I was having a hard time not feeling guilty, so we stopped for lunch and I downed a couple of glasses of wine, and the guilt started to mind its own business. We began talking excitedly about which outfit she would wear next Saturday night, and she even wanted me to borrow some of her new clothes. I happily pretended (to myself) that this was all a great idea.

The following Saturday came, and we were dressed and ready by the time Alex showed up. "Wow, you both look amazing" she blurted out while staring at Lili before she was even through the door. I noticed she was looking at Lili with something that may have resembled lust and I instantly felt a pang of jealousy. Off we went. The party was like all the others I had been to, only this time Lili got paired with someone quite early on and went willingly. She emerged sometime later and smiled a sad smile and told me everything went great. Only a little while later I saw her go to the back room where they were snorting coke and she came back overly energetic. On the way home I asked her how she was doing. She told me she was great, never better. I began to see the sadness in her eyes again. I wanted to say something about the coke, but I didn't have a lot of credibility, since I occasionally did coke as well. I honestly hated to see her spiralling downwards with me. The next day we went out for a few hours and dispersed a smaller chunk of her cash, spent some of it on more clothes and accessories, and then she spent the rest buying drinks for the house at the pub we ended up at. This time she was the one stumbling home with her version of the scruffy man. I played my music so I wouldn't have to hear them in the next room, which would have made me think about my own shit, and I wasn't looking to gain any personal awareness that day.

Chapter 17

On and On

On and on went life. As I look back, it all started to become a bit of a blur. We partied harder, did more coke, loosened our standards, and generally made reckless choices over the course of a few short years. I had become a bit too thin, but was too out of it to notice, but Lili had actually begun to put on some weight. Alex was the first to notice, and she started giving Lili a hard time about it, calling her chubster, telling her to lay off the potato chips, and reminding her that no one wanted to pay to have sex with a fatty. I cringed when Alex spoke to Lili like this. I just assumed the few extra pounds were because she had been drinking a lot, so instead I tried to encourage her to lay off the booze a little. For the first time since she started working with us, Lili declined joining us that Saturday night. I told her she looked fine, but she just shook her head sadly and retreated back to her bedroom.

When I got home that I night I was strung out on coke as usual, and I went and laid in my bed. I thought I heard Lili crying, but I didn't actually give a fuck about anyone but myself at that moment, so I rolled over, put a pillow over my ears, and drifted off to sleep. When I woke up the next morning she wasn't in the apartment, which was weird, she was always in the apartment, or at least told me where she was going. I poured myself a cup of coffee, sat on my porch and tried not to ponder life. Instead, I smoked a few cigarettes and considered what colour to paint my nails. I tidied up a bit around the house, threw a load of laundry in, ate a bowl of cereal, and she still wasn't home. So, I tossed on a pair of sweatpants and a hoodie and went out looking for her. She wasn't at the coffee shop, the pub, the food market, or the dog park. Since I had run out of other ideas, I went to the abandoned building she sometimes went back to when she was sharing her profits. I stepped over the same homeless people shooting up the same heroin, walked past the same sleeping bodies passed out from the same bottles of wine, and heard the same conversations I had heard last time I was here. It was like a snapshot in time, never changing, completely the same, yet the faces were all different. And that's when I saw her. She was crumpled up in the corner looking completely strung out with a needle on the ground beside her and her head in the lap of a filthy drug-addicted woman.

I rushed to her, calling her name, and I began shaking her. The homeless woman startled and looked up at me "Hey lady" she slurred, "get your hands off her, she's mine". I grabbed Lili and picked her up off the floor, mostly carrying her across the room. She felt heavy, but there was no way I was leaving her here. I tried to stand her up, but she just rolled her eyes back and gurgled. I managed to get her down the stairs onto the street and immediately hailed a cab. I ordered the driver to get us to the hospital as fast as possible. I wasn't sure if Lili was going to live. Lili had to live, she was everything to me, she was like my family now, like the little sister I never had, the best friend I'd always wanted. She was truly the only person I had ever trusted. I didn't know what I would do without her.

I was in the waiting room for about an hour before a doctor came in and asked to speak to me. "Lili is awake now. She's asking for you". I turned to walk in, but the doctor grabbed me by the arm abruptly and turned me around. "Wait, there's something you should know".

Chapter 18

Everything Changes

I slowly approached Lili's bed. I wasn't sure if she knew. I met her eyes and she had tears streaming down her face. "Do you know?" she asked. I just nodded. And then the sobbing began. I rushed over to her and sat on her bed holding her, wishing I could take all of her pain away. She was quite hysterical and was muttering between sobs "I don't know how.... It's all my fault.... I deserve to die, I'm such a bad person." She went on like this for a while, ignoring my rebuttals and arguments, telling her it was fine, she was fine, her baby was fine. That just made her sob harder. "I tried to kill my baby" she wailed, now to the point of hyperventilating. "No, Lili, no, your baby's going to be just fine" I promised as I stroked her back and tried to calm her down. I got her to lay down on her side and I continued stroking her back, speaking calmly to her as though she was a child. She eventually drifted off to sleep, and I took the opportunity to step away and speak to the doctor.

The doctor told me that Lili had admitted that she had been at a clinic that morning learning that she was pregnant, and then she had panicked and gone out to get high. She was about 4 months along, and the doctor said it was too early to determine if the drugs would have any long-term effects on the baby. I was in shock. A baby.... what on earth was Lili going to do with a baby? And holy shit, I had let her (encouraged her) to run her life into the ground. She was not equipped to care for an infant. She had no life skills, no way to support herself and a baby other than selling her body. I would just have to support them both. I couldn't let Lili continue in this lifestyle with a child. I had it all worked out, and I went back in the room to tell her.

"Lili?" I called. I assumed she had gone to the bathroom, which surprised me, since she seemed in pretty bad shape. I called again and nothing. I pushed open the bathroom door and it was empty. I was beginning to feel mounting panic.

"Nurse, nurse" I cried frantically and began running down the corridor. I managed to blurt out some jumbled words about Lili being missing as I ran back and forth past the nurse's station. I was quickly apprehended and told that I needed to calm down and take a breath, that we would find her. I wasn't convinced. One nurse got on the phone with someone (possibly security), and I couldn't quite hear what she was saying. "Have they found her? Has anyone found her??" I began to get frantic again.

After about 20 minutes of not finding her, I bolted out of the hospital, knowing I had to find her. I was pretty sure I knew where to look. Off I went again to the abandoned building and climbed up the stairs, dreading what I might see. When I saw her standing in the window, I was relieved. She looked so beautiful standing there with the sunlight streaming in around her – like an angel almost. I smiled and started to walk towards her, gently calling her name. She turned her head slowly to look behind her, smiled beautifully at me while we made brief eye contact, turned back to face the street, then suddenly let go, allowing herself to free fall from the 4th floor window.

Chapter 19

Back on

I went back to work on Monday still in the afterglow of having re-united with Dave. I was feeling on top of the world, like I could take on anything. I spent the day being productive at work and chatting with Dave on the phone when I got home. On Tuesday, he asked me if I would allow him to take me out on a date on Friday. I was thrilled at the idea. And nervous. I knew I didn't have a lot of relationship skills, or even normal sex-life skills. And I did not want a repeat of the last time when the evening ended with me bolting due to my intense aversion to being dominated. At this point I wasn't even sure if I was repairable.

So, to take the pressure off, I decided not to shave my legs before my date. I also went ahead and put on some embarrassingly comfortable and particularly unflattering underclothes – the kind that usually went along with sweatpants night, which generally ended with me sleeping on the couch under a pile of potato chips and candy wrappers.

He picked me up at 6 pm sharp, and when I opened the door, I immediately felt like I had made a terrible choice. He was dressed to the nines, and he looked and smelled amazing. I, on the other hand, was wearing jeans and a t-shirt with my hair pinned up loosely in the back. I began to stammer and back up, thinking I may have time to make a run for my room to re-configure my general presentation. Instead, he pulled me in close, kissed me roughly on the lips, followed by a gentle kiss on the forehead, and then held me at arm's length.

"I'm sorry, I didn't realize we were going somewhere fancy, I should go change...." I tried to pull away.

"Don't be ridiculous, you look amazing" he countered.

"There's just one thing" and he reached up and brushed a loose piece of hair out of my eyes. "Perfect" he announced. I just smiled, knowing that was far from true, and grabbed my purse.

We drove for a while in the comfort of his BMW and eventually pulled up to the Biltmore Hotel. I had heard that their Skytop restaurant was one of the best in town but had never been. Now I was particularly sorry I had worn such shabby underclothes; this was shaping up to be a night I was sure to appreciate and would definitely be inclined to show my appreciation later. We ate, we drank champagne, and we talked. And then we talked some more. He held my hand across the table as we sipped our champagne and shared some laughs, shared more about ourselves, and shared a deepening sense of intimacy. After he paid the bill, he took me by the hand, led me out, and opened the car door for me. Tucked neatly into his car, I began to reflect on what an amazing man Dave was. In fact, maybe too amazing for me. I began to have doubts that he would still want me after finding out about my past. I felt myself begin to shut down and I felt a chill pass through me. I was bracing myself for what would surely be the end of us once he found out my whole story. I had decided earlier that tonight would be the night I told him everything. Now I was having serious second thoughts. We rode in silence for a while as I brooded.

"You're awfully quiet" Dave finally spoke up as he glanced over at me with a look of concern. "You feeling ok?"

"Yeah, maybe I just had a bit too much champagne" was all I was prepared to offer him at the moment. We rode on in silence.

I wasn't sure where he was taking me. Lost in my thoughts, I didn't ask. Eventually I recognized his neighbourhood and wasn't sure what he was up to when we pulled up to his house. He parked the car, unbuckled his seat belt, and turned to look straight at me.

"We're going to go into my house, ok?" I just nodded in return.

"I have the urge to turn you upside down and shake what's bothering you out, but if you're lucky, I'll just ask nicely a few more times until you crack under the pressure" he smiled wryly and jumped out of the car, running around to open my side.

"My lady" he presented his hand, and all I could do was take it and allow myself to be led up to his door. I was seriously considering faking illness or inventing an emergency at this point, but I kept my mouth shut for the time being. He led me inside, invited me to sit down on the couch, and went and hung his suit jacket.

"Do you want anything to drink?" he called from the kitchen. I requested water, as I figured I needed to be on my game so I didn't get tricked into thinking he might actually not leave me once I told him the truth.

As he sat on the couch next to me and took my hand, I gulped nervously. God, I needed a cigarette. I didn't even care that I had long since quit. Maybe I needed more booze. Oh right, I had decided to avoid getting drunk so that I'd have a clear head. Good god how was I going to get through this without a crutch. Maybe I could just forget the conversation and start fucking him immediately. I would just have to reach up ever so smoothly to just past his head where the lamp was, discretely turn it off so I could whip off my disgusting underclothes without him seeing, and promptly mount him. I was almost certain my plan was flawless.

"Cass....Cass" I had zoned out while mentally executing my plan.

"Sorry, yes I'm here". I could see my plan was not coming

together, so I settled on the truth.

"Um...." I began awkwardly, pausing for roughly a minute.

"I'd like to share some.... uh.... stuff about myself with you tonight". I took a deep breath, stared straight ahead, and then went for it. I talked about my childhood, my overprotective and abusive parents, I shared how I met Alex, and then I proceeded to tell him everything about my past as a high-priced call girl, hesitating for a moment before lunging into the part about being a dominatrix. I talked briefly about Lili and shared how everything would eventually fall apart. I just kept talking and talking, not pausing to see how he would react. I was terrified to find out what he would say or do once I finally stopped. As I began winding down, I snuck sideways glances at him through my hair. I noticed that at least he was still there. Also, he was not looking particularly horrified. That had to be a good sign. He reached over to my chin, turned my face gently to face him, and stared into my eyes intently for a few seconds before speaking.

"Cass, your story is both fascinating and tragic. I hate that you have had so much sadness and grief in your life. I'm grateful that you shared it with me tonight and I understand that must have been terrifying. But I want you to know, none of it makes any difference to how I feel about you. That was your past, your story, we all have our history that made us who we are. And frankly, I am completely in love with who you are. Cass, I'm completely in love with you".

I then let him pick me up and carry me to his bedroom. He drew back the sheets, laid me down slowly, and then began to peel away my clothes one by one, telling me the whole time how beautiful I was, how perfect I was. Once he had me completely undressed, he took his own clothes off, laid on the bed beside me, and, in an unprecedented move, just held me. And not once did he mention the atrocious underpants.

Chapter 20

All the Pieces Fall

What I remember next is a sensation of running downstairs in what felt like slow motion while time was elapsing all within a single second. I was calling her name and then hearing my voice echoing around in my head in slow motion, deafening all other sounds and never landing, just swirling and spiralling in my head as I spiralled down the staircase. The moment I burst into the daylight, reality hit me like a punch to the face, knocking me back into a stumble. I nearly fell to the ground, and as I spun around, I saw her. Her lifeless body seemed unreal – like a sad mannequin, a rag doll, a prop someone had thoughtlessly left by the side of the road. I stumbled towards her timidly, this time calling her name gently, as though I could summon her to be alive if I asked nicely. As I drew closer, I began to see the carnage. I keeled over and began throwing up violently. I fell to my knees, dry heaving over the gut-wrenching sounds that were coming from somewhere deep within me. That's the last thing I remember of that day.

I woke up in my bed with my mother standing over me. Oh shit, what kind of shitty-ass trouble had I gotten myself into that my mother had been called to help. She was never any help to me, with her judgmental stares, her preachy tones, and her constant sighing, as though life was altogether too much for her. I pretended I didn't see her and closed my eyes again, hoping she would be gone when I opened them again.

"I saw you open your eyes Cassandra" she chirped, clucking her tongue as though she was already disappointed in me.

"Mother, why are you here? Did I finally go off my rocker and you're here to spoon feed me your religious crap and save me? If that's the case, I'd rather just go fucking insane, so you can leave, I'm sure I'll be fine" I tried, but it came out more like a mouth full of cotton.

"Cassandra, open your eyes, you need to talk to me" she persisted in her annoying "mother knows best" tone.

"Fine, what? Go ahead and tell me - why are you here?" I opened my eyes and met hers straight on with a challenge. That's when I noticed something soft in her eyes. She was looking at me with.... sadness? No....regret? No, it was more like.... oh shit, it was pity. Why was she looking at me with pity? I didn't want to know, I didn't want to think, I didn't want to acknowledge, I, oh shit, it was crashing in on me like a tidal wave of thoughts, emotions, and pure horrified panic.

"Oh my god, oh my god, oh my god, where is she?" I began to scream and struggle to get up. My mother held me down and summoned someone from the other room, who raced in, jabbed my arm with a needle, and laid me back down with a firm strong hand. That's the last thing I remember from that day.

I vaguely recall another time or two of something similar happening, but it was all blurring together. It was, as I was to find out later, a week before I was properly awake and no longer being sedated. That's when the actual hell would begin.

Chapter 21

Living the Dream

I woke up the next morning cradled on my side in Dave's arms. I had never felt so peaceful. I stared at his face for a while. I noticed a small scar on his left eyebrow. I admired his full pouty lips and his strong masculine jawline. I was just reaching up to push a stray lock of hair from his forehead when he opened his eyes and stared sleepily into mine. A smile began to light up his whole face.

"Good morning beautiful" he mumbled, then pulled me in closer, keeping his eyes locked on mine.

"I trust you slept well?" he followed, with a small kiss on my nose. I opened my mouth to answer him, but failed to get any words out, as he suddenly pressed me onto my back, and crushed his mouth down hard on mine. He began probing forcefully into my mouth with his tongue, and I could feel his hardness mounting against my leg. I let out an audible moan, which in turn made him harder as he began to grind his hard cock onto my leg. We were locked in a heated embrace, both panting and gripping each other in a frenzy. He grabbed both of my hands and held them above my head, pressing his lips down harder on mine and shoving his tongue back inside my mouth roughly. I began to squirm and try to get my hands free, and he whispered

"Please Cass, let me make love to you. Let me take you. I want you to be mine." I moaned again and found myself pressing my hips into his.

"Yes. Yes." Was all I could manage to get out.

"Yes what, Cass? What do you want me to do to you?" He looked at me as though staring into my very being, and I felt closer to him than I had every felt with anyone before. I felt like he was looking into my soul, accepting me for who I was, loving me with every ounce of his being.

"Yes Dave, make love to me. Take me, make me yours, I love you, Dave. Take me now, take me hard, I want you now, I want you so ba...." He was kissing me again before I could finish begging him to be inside me.

"I'm going to make love to you Cass....but I'm in no rush" He grinned playfully, and he let go of my wrists, propping himself up on one elbow.

"First, you must be teased". He reached up and brushed the hair off of my forehead and told me again how beautiful I was. He drew the sheets down and looked briefly into my eyes, then let his gaze fall across my body, from head to toe. I felt so exposed, so vulnerable, so wet, and so ready. I heard him exhale as his eyes lingered over me. He drew his eyes back up to make eye contact with me again, then cupped my face in his hand and briefly kissed me on the lips, then slowly let his hand slide down, tenderly caressing my neck, then grazing my throat softly while continuing to make eye contact. Holy shit, I was so turned on, I had never wanting anyone more. His hand trailed further down, and he gently allowed his fingertips to graze my nipple, as though accidentally. I felt a direct pulsing in my pussy, and involuntarily arched my hips up towards him and moaned, as though begging him to touch me, to be inside me. He leaned over me and began softly stroking my nipple with his tongue. Back and forth, with more and more force, while I heaved my chest up towards his mouth in desperation. Finally, he took my whole breast into his mouth and began to suck, while flicking his tongue back and forth across my nipple. I almost came, and he looked up at me and smiled before going back to sucking on my breast, letting his hand brush over my closely shaven mound, tracing his fingers around my upper thighs, my abdomen, and brushing again and again lightly over my mound while I pressed my hips up to meet his fingertips each time, letting out jagged breaths, and sucking in involuntarily. He moved his mouth to my other breast and began to press his fingers ever so gently up and down over the closed lips of my pussy, probing further and further inside, and urging me to separate my legs by pushing my thighs apart. He finally dipped into my throbbing wet pussy and used my wetness to continue teasing and massaging my clit. By this time, I was begging him to hurry up and get inside me, but he was not nearly done teasing me. I closed my eyes and lay my head back onto the pillow, and felt him slide down my body, kissing and licking my abdomen, the top of my mound, and then dragging his wet tongue up my inner thighs. He flicked his tongue ever so lightly over my hot pulsating clit, back and forth, skimming, sliding, poking, kissing, and eventually he rammed his tongue deeply across my clit, then with his whole mouth sucked hard on me while continuing to probe his tongue across my clit repeatedly. He moved his hand down to my wet opening and inserted two fingers, sliding in and out while continuing to feast on my clit. My head was spinning, my hands were gripping the sheets beside me, and I was bucking into him, about to come. That's when he stopped.

"You know what, I think we should talk first" was all he said, then he rolled onto his back and reached over and held my hand.

Chapter 22

Rock Bottom Finds a New Bottom

I awoke to find myself alone in my room. It smelled of coffee, and I could hear someone in the kitchen bustling about humming to themselves.

"Hello" tried to come out of my mouth, but it came out more like "Hhhh" and ended with a croaking sound.

"Hello" I got it out a little louder this time, and suddenly the humming stopped. I heard footsteps approaching my bedroom, and suddenly there was Alex. All tall and gorgeous, hair cascading beautifully around her shoulders, nails manicured to perfection. She was wearing a very chic dress with expensive looking heels and a frilly apron she had found in my kitchen pantry. I wanted to laugh. Or cry. I stared at her until she interrupted my confusion with "What are you staring at? Oh, and I made coffee". She brought me a cup and she sat on my bed and brought me up to speed. I had been in and out of consciousness for the past week, being awake just long enough to eat, drink, and use the washroom, then I would crawl back to bed and cry myself to sleep, or just pass back out. Apparently, Alex had been at the helm, calling in my mother, hiring a full-time nurse, making sure I was "suitably medicated" for my comfort. I was astounded that Alex had done all of this.

"Why?" I had asked her a few times before she explained her reasons.

"Cass, you're really all I have. You are like a sister to me, and I know what Lili meant to you. You were trying to jump out the window when I first arrived here. I just can't lose you..." she looked away and trailed off. "Oh, Cass, I'm so sorry" and Alex began to weep. Sitting there on the side of my bed, we held each other and just cried and cried. We had created such a gigantic mess, and we both felt fully responsible.

I didn't know what to do with myself going forward. I cried because of my loss for Lili, then I cried because I felt responsible. Then I cried because I felt like I had no future and again thought about jumping out of the window.

"What are we going to do Alex? What are we going to do?" I kept sobbing until I was depleted. She got me some water and laid me back down on the bed. I asked her to open the window for some air, and then watched her fumble over the latch, tell me it must be stuck, and assure me that she would have someone look at it. I later found out it had been locked for my safety. Probably not the worst move. I got up a few hours later and attempted to gag down some toast. I threw it up and went and sat at the kitchen table sipping water. I told Alex that my head was pounding and asked her for something for it. She brought me a pill, and within half an hour, I began to feel a wonderful warmth sweep through my body. I felt like none of these problems were insurmountable, and I finally began to smile.

"Hey Alex, what was that you gave me? It was delightful. I may need some more of that when this one wears off!"

The pill she had given me was called Fiorinal. It made all of my pains go away and made everything in the world feel so much better. She left me with the bottle. Over the next few weeks, I noticed that my doses were creeping slightly closer together. It started with one or two a day, and by the end of two weeks they were every four hours. I called her to see if she could get me more, as I was beginning to fear running out of them. She brought me another bottle and told me to be careful, that these were very addictive.

"Don't worry" I assured her; I just needed a little something to get through this rough patch. My mom had long since left, Alex was back to her life, and I was left mostly alone to sort myself out. So how I spent my days was as follows: get up, take a Fiorinal, lay down and wait for it to take effect, roam about looking at stuff with renewed interest in my apartment once it had taken effect. Eat something, watch some TV, and then take another Fiorinal. Shower, rinse, repeat. I believe it took me several bottles and three or four months before I realized I was now a drug addict. I had called Alex begging for more repeatedly, crying, telling her this was the last time, telling her it was the only thing saving my life, telling her she owed it to me after all. So out of guilt, she kept bringing me more. I never asked her where she was getting it from. I just kept taking it as though my very life depended upon it. The fourth month in was around where I finally hit rock bottom.

Chapter 23

Cut Off

Alex stopped by to check on me now and then. I mostly held myself together in her presence. She would call me and tell me she was heading over. I'd take a pill so that I was fit to socialize, and I'd always pour us a drink or two while we visited. I would make certain to remember to put on pants, and almost always remembered to brush my hair. My teeth maybe weren't so lucky. I'm sure my grooming habits were beginning to slide, and there was definitely a time or two when I was wearing pyjamas while we visited. Whenever I realized that I was still wearing pyjamas, I'd just pretend I had slipped back into something more comfortable to hang out on the couch and have girl chat. The only problem was, I was having less and less to say. I felt fidgety in her presence, as though it was her fault that I had to pretend to have my life in order. I believed that I had her fooled. I could never understand why she asked me so many intrusive questions.

Alex finally cut me off. She stopped bringing pills, and she even stopped taking my calls. The morning I woke up and reached for my bottle of pills and my last bottle was empty may have been the new worst day of my life. I was surprised, but mostly devastated, at how new *worst days of my life* just kept surpassing the last worst day. This one beat out my rape day by a long shot. This one even topped seeing my best friend splattered on the sidewalk. This one involved me in a full-blown withdrawal panic over running out of my pleasure-demon, the one thing I had grown to love more than anything and anyone else, including myself and the very act of being alive. There was no time for hair brushing. There was certainly no time for teeth brushing. Pyjamas were close enough. I already knew where I needed to go. Life was beginning to feel like it was coming full circle. I could hardly believe I was willing to go back there, back to the one place that had haunted my nightmares endlessly for the past four months.

I began to mount the steps. It was darker than I remembered. And smelled much worse. And my head hurt a lot. I stopped to throw up a bit. Either from the stench, or possibly because I was in a such terrible withdraw. I kept climbing. I stepped over a person. It didn't even dawn on me to wonder whether or not they were alive. It really didn't matter to me at all. I threw up again while stepping around a hunched-over form. Some of it probably landed on them. Again, none of this was relevant to me. My ears were beginning to ring, and I was feeling dizzy. As I surfaced onto the upper floor of the building I began to stumble and was having trouble seeing clearly. I stopped to fully throw up and I remember being slightly alarmed somewhere way in the back of my mind that I felt no shame or embarrassment whatsoever.

I sat down beside a man who was crumpled up in over-sized clothes with needles and vials dropped to the floor beside him, his empty hand outreached, as though he was still holding his favourite possession, his head cocked to one side, mouth open, eyes unfocused but staring straight ahead. He did not see me at first. I just sat with him for a while. Finally, he acknowledged me with a nod, asking me what I had for him. I showed him some cash and he took my arm. He asked if this was my first time. I only nodded.

After about 30 seconds I let out a deep sigh, leaned back, and had never felt so comforted. There was a calmness about me that I had never felt before. I knew that life was ok, better than ok, life was perfect. This blissful euphoric state lasted several hours. I had long since left the warehouse and made my way back to my apartment, where I sat on my balcony and smoked cigarettes. I threw up a few times, presumably from the combination, but it didn't stop me an hour later from smoking another cigarette. I was starting to think that maybe, just maybe I could actually get my shit back together. I was feeling pretty optimistic actually; I knew that I could live without the drugs, I could get a decent job again, and I could begin to make something of my life.

And then I began to come down.

Chapter 24

Actual Hell

For a while I felt ok while I was coming down. I had been lounging on my patio for hours in an almost nap-like state, my mind drifting, then floating. Eventually my mind slowly began to become more and more aware of my surroundings. I first noticed that I was getting chilly. Then I started becoming acutely aware of the stiffness in my neck and back from the position I had been reclined in for four or five hours. I tried to get up to go to my bed, but immediately sat back down with a sudden wave of nausea and all-over aching. I sat for a few minutes, my head in my hands, trying to get my head clear enough to move to my bedroom. I stood up again, this time wasn't any easier. I felt drained and defeated. I felt angry that no one had thought to bring me inside. I thought about that again until I realized I had no one to take care of me. I stumbled inside and began to look around for something that would calm my stomach. I figured I'd have some antacid or anti-nausea tablets somewhere, but I was turning up nothing useful. I thought about eating a small snack, but my stomach lurched at the thought. I made the choice to leave my apartment with the pretence that I was going to head to the drug store. I did not. Instead, I headed to the drug warehouse.

In my agitated and achy state, I had very little trouble convincing myself that I should take another very small dose of heroin just to take the edge off so I could think straight. I wasn't, after all, prepared for the come down. I would simply take a small amount to get back the clarity I had felt while high, then I could go to the drug store, stock up on items that I would need while coming down, and then I could go home and resume my old life as a non-addict. All of this was thoroughly and convincingly thought out in the span of 3 or 4 seconds.

I felt myself walking back towards the warehouse even before the 4 seconds of bullshit that I passed off as logic finished crossing my mind. I climbed the steps. I found a junkie. I put out money. I got high. I went home. I then repeated this roughly 60 times over the next few months. Then I ran out of money. I needed a new plan. My new plan was as follows: climb the steps, find a junkie, put out, get high, go home. That only worked a few times. Then they wanted money again. So I descended the steps, went out to the street, and stumbled several blocks up to where the hookers hung out. This wasn't a stretch, right? I mean, I had sold my body many times before. Mind you, it had been for thousands of dollars at a time, and I had been completely in charge most of the time. This time was different. This time was way different.

At first I hung back, not sure how to pursue the john. I watched a few girls approach cars, do the typical lean-in, and then sooner or later hop into a car and speed off. I eventually approached my first car. As I went to knock on the window, it suddenly came whizzing down with a feeling of urgency.

"Get in, well get in, hurry up, get in God damn it!". I was surprised but followed his instruction. I was soon sitting beside a flabby man in his early 40's with rumpled hair and khakis. His pants were pulled up too high and his shirt was awkwardly tucked in. Even in my worn-out state I could see the disgustingness of this man. I didn't care; to me he represented quick cash...and the quicker the better. I was reminded why hookers put on such a show...oohing and aahing, faking orgasms, acting like this was the best damn fuck they had ever had. Quicker was definitely better.

We didn't even bother with a hotel room. Apparently, we

were going to do this in his car. First, he grabbed my head and smashed it down on his dick, mashing my face in so hard I could barely get his dick in my mouth. I managed at last to get the tip in and was soon choking because he had me shoved down so hard. He then began pulling me up and down by the hair. After a minute or two he shot his load down my throat and still held me there. After a good five minutes of trying not to gag on his flaccid cock, he began shoving me up and down by the hair again. His boner began pulsating in my mouth once more, and this time he was ready for the real thing. He yanked me up by the hair with one hand and slapped me across the face with the other. He began shouting obscenities and insults at me and told me to shut the fuck up when I began to protest. I was promptly informed that I was nothing more than I low-life slut, I deserved to get fucked hard, and then maybe even choked to death if he was in the mood. Oh god, please tell me he was not in the mood. Instead, he shoved my face down in the passenger's seat, spread my ass cheeks, and began trying to shove his cock in my ass. When it wouldn't go, he got angry and began beating me. He was slapping my ass, punching my back, scratching me, and then spit on me in disgust. He grabbed my ass again, this time shoving harder, and finally managed to rip into me. After what felt like an hour of raw painful cramping ass-fucking, he finally came again, this time with a punch to my back and a shove of my head into the car door. He leaned over and opened the car door, gathered up what he could reach of my clothes and shoved me out, throwing my clothes on top of me. He laughed. Then he threw a fifty-dollar bill at me, slammed the door shut, and sped off. I was lost. Literally.

I yanked on what he had left me of my clothes. Luckily, this included pants and a t-shirt. No underclothes, but at least I was covered. I had no idea that I was also sporting a fat lip and the beginnings of some violent bruising. I was enraged for a minute. Then I remembered what I was out here for. Back on the main street I flagged down another car, and the gentleman invited me in. I told him I needed a ride. He told me he needed a blowjob. We had a deal. I gave him a blowjob with my swollen and sore mouth. He gave me a ride back to the warehouse. I climbed the stairs. I found a junkie. I paid. I got high.

Chapter 25

Time Flies

The rest of the world ceased to exist for me over the next several months. I got the hang of street hooking pretty fast. I managed to stay away from the pimps and avoid the majority of the violent johns. It didn't take a lot of shitty experiences to learn what type of guy I was willing to "date". I preferred the low self-esteem, apologetic desperate men, who just visited now and then because they needed some quick and attachment-free sexual release, or the lonely married men who hoped their wives and children never found out. They were quick, paid fairly, and tended to be overly polite. I never really thought much about what I was doing or the possibility of getting cleaned up. My own self esteem had dropped to where this all seemed ok. I felt so shitty about being a low-life hooker that I did more heroin. I turned more tricks so I could continue being a low-life heroin addict. This was a vicious circle I felt destined to spin in until it killed me, or I, myself, leaped from a warehouse window.

I was coming up on the one-year anniversary of Lili's death. I had not seen Alex since the last day she brought me pills. When she refused to bring me more pills, I refused to see her. She told me I could rot in hell for all she cared. Well, luckily for her, that's exactly what I had been doing. I was dazed out in my apartment, and was debating whether to eat KD for dinner, or shoot up heroin when my phone rang. I was surprised – it didn't ring very often anymore.

"Hello". There was a silence on the other end, then an audible sigh.

"Hello...ok, whoever you are, I don't have time for this shit." I was just about to hang up when I heard "Cass, don't hang up". I hung up. I seem to recall her telling me I was dead to her...or maybe that she was dead to me. At any rate, she had made it clear she was washing her hands of me now that I had become useless to her. I'm sure she had moved on to other youthful naive girls with an axe to grind and an urge to punish their parents by making bad choices. The phone rang again. I wondered what she could possibly want to say to me. Then a small part of me thought maybe she could hook me up with some high paying jobs, or at least a hit, so I relented and answered the phone.

"What?" I blurted sharply. Alex quickly replied,

"Cass, please don't hang up." She waited a few seconds to see if I would, and when she was satisfied that she could still hear me breathing, she pressed on.

"Cass, I'm sorry. I'm sorry for bringing you the pills. I'm sorry for bailing on you when you became addicted. I'm sorry for leaving you to rot in hell and acting like I no longer cared."

She began to sob. I just listened and thought "This is pathetic, it's kind of bringing me down. I wonder, if I hung up and left the house now, how soon would it be until I could score".

She went on about how at first, she didn't know what to do with me, then she was worried about being an enabler, and felt guilty for having started me on the pills. Then she convinced herself that tough love was best, and that she should let me hit rock bottom. She told me that she often spoke to people that knew me so she could check up on me now and then. She knew that I had become addicted to heroin and was turning tricks on the street. What she didn't know, I was certain, was how I felt dead inside. She didn't know that I felt worthless, useless, and undeserving of being alive. She didn't know that I had miserably failed at overdosing two times because I was too much of a chicken shit to do it like I meant it. She didn't know that one side of me desperately wanted to see her, but the rest of me just wanted to quit listening to her whiny shrill voice and go get high. Or she may have known these things.

"So, what do you say, Cass? Will you meet me? I can come to you, or you can stop by my place for a coffee, anything you want, what do you say?"

I paused. Then I sighed deeply. I opened my mouth to tell her to go fuck herself and instead heard myself agreeing to meet her at her place for coffee the next day. When I walked in, I froze, spun around, and began heading back down the steps hastily. She caught up with me, grabbing my arm. I yanked it away and began yelling at her,

"How dare you! You brought me here to embarrass me and humiliate me in front of my family? Let go of me!"

She would not let go. Instead, she held tight, and told me that she was not letting go. She had got me into this mess, she was prepared to do what she had to get me out. I screamed and lurched away, but she was much stronger than I was, especially in my current strung-out state.

"Look Cass, you can follow me back in, or I will throw you over my shoulder and haul your pathetic ass back into that house. One way or the other, you're going back in there!" She stood and stared at me; eyebrows raised in a challenge.

"Fine, I'll go into your stupid place and be humiliated if that will make you happy" I shouted, but this time with somewhat less authority. I allowed her to drag me back in, where she sat me in a chair while a circle of my family and old friends sat staring ruefully at me. This was going to be a long night.

Chapter 26

Sex in the Morning? Yes Please

Oh my god! What could Dave possibly want to talk about right now? Right when I'm about to come from the most glorious pussy eating I had ever experienced!

"Please, can't you finish? Please? I'm so close right now, just a little more, then we'll talk, I promise" and I began pulling his hand towards my wet throbbing tortured pussy and tried to get him to keep touching me. He pulled away gently and rolled onto his side.

"Look at me Cass. Please." His voice was so sweet, so vulnerable. I turned and looked at him. I tried to hide my disappointment and put on a semi-warm smile, in an effort to hide the incredible amount of frustration I was currently feeling.

"So, you know how we've talked about having an open and honest relationship? How we want to be able to tell each other anything and everything? How you opened up to me and I accepted you for exactly who you are and what you've been through?" I nodded, starting to go numb, my mind racing, wondering what the fuck he was about to tell me.

"It's just that.... Cass, you know I love you, right?"

"Yes Dave, yes, of course I do" I tried to sound calm, but felt icy and terrified on the inside. I stared at him as he turned his face to stare up at the ceiling, biting his lower lip and frowning slightly. I waited for a very long 30 seconds while my mind raced. Did he want to break up, was he seeing someone else, was he dying of cancer, was he some sort of pervert that needed strange fetishes to get off? I was about to yell "Well get on with it!" when he turned back towards me, reached out to my face, stroking my cheek gently with the back of his hand, and began to speak:

"Cass, I love you more than I thought possible. I loved you before you shared your story with me. I love you even more now, even though I didn't know that was possible. We've both made mistakes, but I know that all of that is behind us now. Cass, I want to do this with you. I mean all of this. I want you. I want to marry you, have children with you, live in the suburbs with you, take our kids to little league, watch our children grow, build a nest egg, grow old together.... Cass, I want it all." He stopped talking and stared at me, holding his breath; a look of fear crept over his face.

"Oh God, I've said too much. Cass, I'm sorry, I shouldn't have. Ignore all that...Cass, you look terrified. I'm sorry, talk to me, please."

I found myself stumbling out of bed and tripping across the room, half holding the sheet as though being modest might make me feel less vulnerable.

"I....I....uh...." I began to sputter from the bathroom. "I just need a minute" I called, trying not to let him hear the trembling in my voice. I looked in the mirror. I saw my face, I was pure white, a wild look in my eyes, my jaw slack and drawn back. I looked like I'd seen a ghost. I looked like a ghost. I backed away from the mirror and slid to the floor hugging my knees to my chest. Tears began to trace down my cheeks. One thousand thoughts filled my head like a runaway train:

He's too good for me, how could I ever be capable of looking after another human? I'd never be a good role model, I'm broken and beyond all repair, he didn't mean it, it's a trick... and on and on and on, the thoughts kept running in circles, having their way with me, leaving me tortured and broken. I sat on the floor feeling depleted, empty and unworthy. I was crying softly and holding my head in my hands when I felt a warm touch on my head.

"Cass come back to bed", which I ignored, as I brushed his hand off.

"Cass, I'm now going to pick you up and bring you back to bed, is that ok?" I nodded one small nod, which was enough encouragement. He leaned over, wrapped his arms around my naked body, and scooped me up effortlessly, carrying me back to the bed, while I crept my arms around his neck, sniffled, and nuzzled my face into his chest. Damn, he smelled good. He laid me down and then sat on the bed looking down at me. He stared at me for a while. I stared back at him. Then I began to giggle. That's when he got a very serious look on his face. Oh shit, maybe I've finally pissed him off for good.

Without missing a beat, he grabbed both of my wrists in his hands, pressed them into the bed above my head, and kissed me so hard I bit my lip a little. I began to buck up into him as he rolled on top of me, pressing his impressive erection into me until it hurt. He was grinding me as though he was completely out of his mind and out of control. When I got a breath, I begged:

"Fuck me Dave, fuck me now and fuck me hard, just fuck me!" He pulled back suddenly and informed me that he was definitely NOT going to fuck me. He firmly told me he was NEVER going to fuck me, and that he was definitely, absolutely going to make love to me over and over and over again tonight, and for the rest of my life. I just smiled. It was a goofy grin, and I couldn't stop, but I really didn't care. I was about to be made love to for the first time in my life. All I could think was:

"Don't fuck this up Cass!"

Chapter 27

The Big Event

Dave drew back and stared into my eyes for several seconds, still holding my wrists. He realized how tightly he was holding me and let go, cocking his head to one side. "You know Cass, you are extraordinarily beautiful". I just smiled, blinked a few times, and whispered, "Thank you". He leaned up on one arm and drew his other hand lightly down my breasts, slowly circling my nipples with his fingertips while staring intently at me. I held his gaze. He began to roll my nipples between his fingers and thumbs, applying more and more pressure until an involuntary moan escaped my lips. He looked very pleased with himself.

"Oh, you like that do you?" He coaxed playfully. I just nodded, holding his gaze. He pinched my nipples a little harder, then bent over and again took one of my erect nipples into his mouth. His warm mouth sucked while his tongue flicked back and forth, bringing me to near ecstasy. He released the nipple and immediately began on the other one. Sucking, flicking and tugging with his mouth, while his hand found my other nipple and began twisting and pinching. I opened my mouth to let out another moan when he moved his mouth onto mine, probing his tongue deep within my mouth, running his tongue up and down mine, then sucking on my tongue gently. His hand began to drift down my body and caress my abdomen, getting closer and closer to my eager pussy, teasing me around the edges, running his hand lightly over my mound. I was trying to rise up to meet his hand, I wanted him to feel how wet I was, how my pussy was throbbing for him, but instead, he flipped me over suddenly and spread my legs with his knee. I was treated to back caresses that crept perilously closer and closer to my wet pussy. His hands began to slide around my hips, and he raised my ass up just enough to slide his tongue across my ass. I felt electric shocks through my body. I tried to turn over, but he held me firm, this time probing deeper with his tongue. He slid his hands up to my breasts and began pulling hard on my nipples while continuing to lick my ass. I was completely unable to control my moaning and breathing by this time, I felt like I could come at any time. He still hadn't touched my pussy when he flipped me back over and grabbed his massive cock in his hand telling me how much he wanted to be inside me. He stroked his cock a few times, and then shimmied up the bed until he could slide his throbbing cock into my mouth. I opened my mouth as wide as I could to take him in. He slid himself so deep into the back of my throat that I nearly gagged, but I was loving seeing him whipped into such a frenzy. I opened my eyes and made eye contact with him while he slid himself in and out slowly. He began to close his eyes and drop his head back.

"Oh yeah Cass, suck my cock, suck it hard. Oh my god, I could come in your mouth right now!" He pulled out abruptly and slid back down me. I knew I wanted him inside me more than I had ever wanted anything. I begged him to be inside me, clawing at his back and trying to grab his cock.

"Lay still Cass, I want this to be slow and I want you to be fully present, right here with me. With that, he kissed me tenderly on the lips, grabbed his rock-hard cock and, while staring deeply into my eyes, slowly began to push inside me. When he got almost all the way in, he breathed out "I love you Cass" as he pushed hard inside me, making me almost bite his tongue when he bent down and kissed me with a violent urgency. He continued to push slowly in and then all the way out, pause, and then slide quickly back in, each time eliciting a frantic moan from my lips. I opened my mouth to tell him how much I loved him, and as I began to say "I love you Dave" I felt my body begin to flutter, the warm feelings flooding up from my pussy and radiating out to the rest of my body, I was wracked with orgasms, one after the other, in a continuous string of release, as I repeated over and over that I loved him. I clawed at his back and nearly lost consciousness. Suddenly Dave blew his load so hard into me it hurt and felt amazing at the same time. He was jerking and crying out with his eyes closed and his hands clenched into fists. He finally began to regain awareness and looked down at me. I was smiling and sleepy.

"So, Cass, do you think we can do that again?"

"Yes please". We fell back asleep feeling extremely peaceful wrapped in each other's arms.

Chapter 28

Intervention

I stared around the room. Well, I more glared around the room. Which was to be expected. No one ever showed up to their own intervention with a delighted disposition. I felt very strongly about wanting to carry on slowly killing my self, my body, my soul, and the last of my spirit and dignity with drugs and prostitution. I was pretty committed to it in a big way. I crossed my arms and stared down at my feet, pondering the odd assortment of people that had shown up. My mom was there, dabbing at her eyes and blowing her nose with a flourish as though we all ought to notice how much trouble and strife this whole affair had been causing her. My dad sat with a glazed-over look on his face, looking nervous that someone would ask him to participate or have something, or anything at all, to say. My older sister Janice, whom I hadn't seen in 3 years, was there, ushering her two young children out of the room, as though being near me might taint them or somehow influence them into becoming a low-life scum, just like their aunt. For a second, I felt a wave of regret slide over me. I had only seen my nieces a few times when they were still babies, they now had to be four and six. They were cute little moppets, with their dark locks hanging nearly down to their waists, their short bangs framing their innocent little faces, their chubby little cheeks. Suddenly I had an overwhelming urge to run over and snatch them up and hug them close, squeezing them until they shrieked, tickling them until they giggled, and kissing them all over those cute little faces. I leaped out of my chair and made a quick start towards them, but Janice's husband Brian had them scooped up and swung them out of the room before I could get close.

"I just wanted.... I wanted to.... can I? I just.........I wanted...." I turned and looked at a room full of eyes staring at me like I was a lion that had escaped in the zoo, and no one wanted to be the first to move.

"Oh, settle down you bunch of assholes! I just wanted to see my nieces. Did you see how cute they are? DID YOU?" I began shrieking that I just wanted to see my nieces and was flailing and swinging at whatever was close to me when I felt strong hands grabbing my arms and guiding me back to my chair. I didn't recognize the two men who had a hold of me.

"Who the hell are you guys? And get your fucking hands off me!" I wrenched away from them as though I had some sort of dignity to maintain. "I'll sit down, now leave me alone you sick perverts. God, I didn't say you could touch me. Do you think you can do whatever you want to me? DO YOU?? I suppose you're going to try to fuck me next? Right here in front of my mom and dad!" I sat down in a dramatic huff and went back to crossing my arms and staring down at my feet. I was coming down so hard now that the room was spinning. I had only meant to stop at Alex's house for a few minutes on my way to getting a fix. I had been running low lately and was feeling desperate, which was partly why I agreed to go to her house in the first place.

The guys backed away and sat down. Then a woman who I didn't recognize began to speak. She was sitting between a couple of old high school friends that I had long since lost touch with who looked terrified to be there.

"Cass, welcome. Thank you for being here". It's not really like I had a choice. Was she some kind of idiot?

"My name is Cecilia" she went on. "I am an intervention specialist. I'm here to help". I hated her. I hated her soft soothing voice. I hated her grey wavy hair and pleated tan slacks. I hated the calm soothing look on her face. I had the urge to get up and punch her in the mouth when she spoke. This was such a joke. I looked around the room again, squinting at everyone suspiciously. I didn't even care about most of these people. It was as though they were saying "Look, we really couldn't find anyone who actually cares about you, so we wrangled up some people that you know, or knew at one time. I was disgusted by the whole thing. I thought the effort was pathetic and insulting. I didn't want to be here. I was wholly consumed with the idea of getting my next fix. I had successfully managed to tune everyone out for a while, and when I came back to my present situation, the annoying lady was just passing the floor off to my mother. Good God, what kind of crap was going to come out of her mouth? She drivelled on for a while, as I half listened to her heaving and moaning about how I had ruined my life and made hers miserable as well. Well, frankly, I couldn't give a shit if she wanted to go fuck herself. My head was starting to pound, and I was finding it extremely hot inside Alex's house. I asked for the window to be opened. And to have a glass of water. I was dying in there. But I wasn't quite sure I could get away with trying to leave. I knew Alex was about the most determined person I had ever known, and she was watching me like a hawk. Next my dad spoke. It sounded roughly like "blah blah blah Cass, shame on you, blah blah blah, making your mother miserable, how could you? Blabbity blah blah blah. You're a bad person and we all hate you and you should go rot in hell". He didn't say those exact words mind you, but his look said something of the sort.

Then Cecilia asked my sister to talk. I was actually surprised to see her here, but strangely riveted by her when she began to speak. I hadn't seen her for so long, and to be honest, I kind of missed her all of a sudden. As kids, we played together all the time, and I had always looked up to her. She had my back in the school yard, she took my side when my parents were breathing down my neck, and she taught me how to kiss boys, put on makeup, and smoke my fist cigarette. Janice had gotten married soon after she graduated – obviously to get out of our parents' house as soon as possible, and for some reason we pretty much lost touch shortly after she started to have babies and I started to sell my body for money.

"Cass......" Janice just stared at me, sighing, her eyes looking sad and tired. "Cass, what happened?" She began to cry openly and told me she was sorry for bailing on me, for leaving me behind, for moving on with her life and forgetting about her little sister.

"No, Janice, no, it wasn't you. I was now crying too, and she came and sat beside me on the couch. She cradled me in her arms and rocked me gently, stroking my hair, telling me how much she loved me and wanted me back in her life. She told me all about my beautiful nieces, how they needed an auntie they could have fun with and look up to. She asked me if I wanted to be that auntie for them. I nodded and brushed away my tears with the back of my hand.

"I'm tired Janice. I'm just so tired".

I relented that day. I surrendered to my addiction and gave up the fight. I agreed to put myself into their hands and they arranged for me to go directly to treatment. I found myself in the back seat of a car with my sister holding my hand and Cecilia driving us to the treatment centre that Alex had pre-arranged and paid for. Janice walked me up to the intake door, kissed me on the forehead, and said "Cass, I love you. I am sorry for all of the tough times you've had, all the challenges that are coming, and that I was not there to help you sooner. I'm here for you now. I'm going to help you through this. And then you will come back to us and be the most amazing auntie that those girls could ever ask for". I walked in and felt the door slam behind me.

Chapter 29

Long Slow Crawl

The crawl back was slow. And long. There was nothing glamorous about this treatment centre. They offered me Methadone to bring me off of my dependency. I declined. It was out of sheer stubbornness and certainty that I had what it took to kick this flat out. For about a week I was in and out of consciousness, a writhing pain worming its way through my body, cold sweats, throwing up on myself, plus I'm pretty sure I wet myself a few times. The staff was fast, efficient, and did the job they were there for. No more, no less. I got no handholding, no sympathetic gestures, but no judgement overall. It was all highly clinical from what I can recall, and it was most definitely the new worst week of my life.

I began to emerge somewhere into the second week. I had longer periods of lucidity and breaks in my agonizing flu-like symptoms that wracked my brain, my body, and my will to live. Looking back, I am grateful that they kept me in a locked and safe environment for the first few weeks. I got daily visits from the doctor, as she checked my vitals, asked me a few questions, and noted my charts. She told me I was doing well under the circumstances and was right on track as far as detoxing went. And that the only thing between me and recovery was time and commitment to full treatment. I barely heard her words at the time, but as I began to have longer periods of clarity, her words began to swirl around in my head, giving me something to chew on besides the constant pain and discomfort that I was in.

It was about two weeks before they moved me to another ward. They came and got me, helped me collect my stuff, and escorted me to a different wing of the treatment centre. We were buzzed in, and the first thing I noticed was the noise. I had been in a room with just myself, my monitoring machines, and the odd quiet voice of the staff for over two weeks. This was overwhelming and making me angry. They brought me into a bedroom that housed four beds and pointed me towards mine. They told me to arrange my stuff any way I liked in my dresser and make myself at home. Really? I didn't see that happening. I sat down on the bed they had pointed to and sunk my head into my hands, falling backwards onto the bed. I had my eyes closed and was hoping all of this would go away when I opened them, but instead a shrill annoying voice pierced the room and sounded like a jackhammer in my brain.

"Heyyyy, look, we got a new one". The voice trailed back out of the room and I could unfortunately hear it all the way down the hall enthusiastically calling god knows who back to the room.

"Shit" I slowly sat up and looked around. I saw that I would be the fourth resident in the small room and that my solitude was now a thing of the past. I stood up slowly, edged towards the door, and peeked out. I didn't see the annoying over-enthusiastic roommate anywhere, so I made a dash for the nurse's station.

"Hello....hello, anyone here?"

A nurse wandered around the corner "Oh hello dear, you must be the new girl. Welcome, my name is Patricia".

Ok, whatever, I wasn't really interested in Patricia, but I figured I needed to play nicely to get what I wanted.

"Hello Patricia, so nice to meet you.... there seems to be a slight misunderstanding. You see, I have been taken to a room that three other women already occupy.... and....well, I just think I'm more suited to a private room.

Patricia took off her reading glasses and peered over her

nose at me "Honey, everyone here thinks they deserve a private room. But that's just not how it works. All of the rooms are shared. Nothing you can do about it, so you best be getting back in there and making nice with your new roommates." She peered back down the hall towards my room. "Well, look at that, what perfect timing, your new roommates are just coming back from group. What a great time to meet them all." And with that she smiled sweetly at me and looked back and forth between me and the room down the hall that I was destined for with one eyebrow raised. I was quite certain this next phase would somehow prove to be worse than the detoxing. I didn't want to play nicely with others.

Chapter 30

Playing Nicely with Others

I sulked back towards the room, shoulders slumped over, staring at the floor, realizing that poking my eyes out seemed less torturous than what I was walking into. I stopped just before the door, took a deep breath, raised my head, forced on a smile, and marched into the room like I owned the place. What the hell, let's show these bitches who's who.

"Good afternoon ladies" I piped up in a horridly upbeat voice. I smiled around the room, opting to put on a show of false bravado instead of letting them see the weak broken fool that I actually was. No sense letting any of them in, I wouldn't be here long. I knew that once I finished detoxing, I would be able to get out of here and get my life back together straight away. I had simply made a few bad choices, no big deal. Easy to fix.

"Well, helloooooo roomie!" The Shrill One started in on me right away. "So, what's your name? Where are you from? What are you in for? How do you feeeeel?" She was practically foaming at the mouth in anticipation of finding out more about "New Girl".

"Cass. From around here. Heroin. And fine. Pretty good, detox wasn't so bad, I should be out of here in no time." And with that, I breezed past them and began to unpack my stuff into the dresser beside my bed like I was delighted to be checking into a five-star hotel.

"I just need a few minutes to get organized, why don't I

meet you all at dinner later" I continued, smiling coldly at them. They looked at me a bit funny, heads tilted to the side, as though I'd make more sense from another angle.

"Well, suit yourself, I guess we'll leave you to it. But don't think we won't drag more out of you later!" And they bustled out of the room, bumping into one another, swearing playfully at each other, and breaking into giggles. Oh boy. This was going to be a regular slumber party. Maybe I could find a very long sheet and kill myself before they returned. I wasn't seriously considering that of course. Not really.

I shoved the rest of my stuff in the drawer quickly and flopped down on the bed, closing my eyes. My head was beginning to hurt from moving around so much and interacting with people and I immediately started daydreaming about getting a fix. My ability to deal with stress had been reduced to nothing, I had no coping skills, I had no plan, I had no life. Oh shit, I draped my arm over my eyes and began to tear up. I rolled over and began to sob into my pillow, getting louder and louder, until I forgot all about my facade of being strong and capable. I really let it go, I mean, I wailed and wailed, drowning out anything that may have been going on around me. I sobbed until my snot was pooling up around my face on the pillow. I sobbed until my head pounded and I could feel my pulse in my forehead. I sobbed until I ran out of sobs. Then I lay limp, sniffling and taking short breaths, picking at the bedspread with my dangling fingertips. I became aware of someone else's presence in the room.

"Who's there?" I mumbled into my pillow.

"It's me Cass, open your eyes."

Chapter 31

The Slow Rebuild

I rolled over and drew my arm away from my face slowly. I swiped at my eyes to get a better look at the figure standing over me. I hadn't even realized I could have visitors here. Slowly Alex started to come into focus.

"So, how's the food here?" She chuckled at herself. I sniffled a little, and she passed me a tissue. I blew my nose for a while, propped up on one elbow, and then just flopped onto my back, as I realized I didn't even have the energy to sit up.

"What are you doing here?" I asked petulantly, a pouty look creeping over my face. "I didn't know people could just pop by. And how long have you been standing there anyways?"

"Cass, I'm allowed to come, as I'm listed as one of your primary contacts. I registered you, paid for you, and filled them in on most of your history. Your sister and I are both considered "pre-approved" visitors. And I've been here witnessing most of your blubbering I'm guessing. I figured you needed to get it all out, so I waited patiently.

"Gee thanks. I was afraid I had a shred of dignity left".

"Hehe, nope" she fired back while shaking her head back and forth. "Not really the place for dignity Cass. I'm guessing they hand it back to you on your way out."

We chatted for a few more minutes. She told me she had just wanted to stop by and check in on me. Make sure I hadn't made a run for it yet. And then in a serious tone she told me she loved me, she supported me, and she had my back all the way to the end of this. And that she had total confidence in me that I would beat this. I was way too stubborn, after all, she was quick to point out. It was really nice seeing her. After she left, I found myself wishing for a friend on the inside. Maybe...just maybe my roommates would not turn out to be too horrible to bear. One could hope.

I slowly sat up, noticed I was dizzy, and called for a nurse with my call button. Patricia pushed into the room all business and concern and seemed relieved to see I only needed some water and help to the bathroom.

"You ok in there honey?" She called through the door.

"Yeah" I croaked back, "I'll be right out". She made sure I finished my water and checked my vitals. "You seem better now, you gonna be ok if I leave?"

"I'm feeling much better, thank you Patricia." I even managed to offer her a genuine smile before she left the room. Ok, maybe I could do this...maybe I could start "peopling".

I noticed that my stomach was starting to growl, which was a good sign. I hadn't been hungry in ages. I made my way towards the dining room timidly, stopping and peeking around the corner so I would know what to expect before I committed to going in. Inside I saw lots of large round tables, and some long picnic style tables, forcing everyone to eat in groups. People were buzzing, moving about, walking towards tables with trays, nodding and smiling at each other, making room for others to sit down. It all seemed too friendly. And scary. I felt frozen there, unable to move from my place, peeking around a corner like the new girl on the first day of school. I suddenly felt a warm hand on my shoulder. I turned around – it was the annoying roommate.

"Sweetie come on in", she spoke softly and looked me right in the eyes.

"You can sit with us – we're right over here". And with that, she guided me quickly over to the rest of the girls, who were sitting at a round table with a few other women I didn't recognize. She told me her name was Jenny, and she introduced me to the crowd. They all waved and mumbled hi with their mouths full.

"Come on, I'll show you what's good and what to steer clear of!" And she led me off to the cafeteria line up. Once I was back at the table, seated and eating my food, I started to relax and look around a bit. I was surprised at how good the food tasted. I had chicken, mashed potatoes, and vegetables on my plate. Plus, I had grabbed a brownie out of sheer greed. I suddenly felt like I hadn't enjoyed food for years. This food was actually pretty fucking amazing. I was so engrossed in my food, that I was surprised whenever I realized that someone had been talking to me, asking me more about myself.

"Mmm, uh huh, yeah" I mumbled between bites. I eventually noticed that the other girls were looking at me and smiling and looking at each other with nods and raised eyebrows.

"What? What are you all staring at? Am I so funny? Oohs look at the new girl, she's so pathetic. Look at the new girl, she's such a loser, she'll never make it. Is that what you're all thinking?" I had dropped my fork, stood up, and was shouting this at them, much to their horror.

"Oh my goodness Cass, no!" Jenny looked stricken. She was shaking her head slowly, repeating "No, no, of course not", her eyes wide. She looked like she might cry. I almost felt sorry for her. I looked back and forth at all the girls at my table. They were all looking at me with kindness and love, telling me they thought I was amazing, that they loved watching my zest for the food, that it reminded them of when they first arrived and hadn't tasted a good meal in ages. They told me that they loved me. That they supported me. That they all stood for me succeeding. That had to be bullshit. Right? These assholes just met me. How could they love me? Fuck, I didn't even love myself. This was bullshit. It had to be. It had to be. It had to be.

Turns out it wasn't.

Chapter 32

Group

The next day I was asked to join group. Ten of us sat in a circle facing each other and the group leader Carol. She was an older, distinguished woman who looked organized and friendly. After welcoming everyone she made a bit of a deal of having me introduce myself. I was asked to state my name, my addiction (or addictions) of choice, the last time I had used, and anything else I wanted to share about myself. After I summed my miserable life up, she went around the room having everyone else state their name, addictions, and last date of using. Since this was a 28-day program, starting with a one-to-two-week detox, everyone had used within the past 6 weeks. Speaking of using, I thought.... I could use a fix right now.

Eventually we finished our introductions, and our talk today was about friends and influences on the outside. I would soon learn that each day we covered different topics. We went around the group asking questions, sharing opinions, and generally trying to sort out how to be with people without using once we were out. For most of us it would mean choosing a whole new set of people to associate with. That shouldn't be hard, since I was pretty much a loner anyways. Oh shit, as we talked it started dawning on me that I would have to make it on the outside. Fuck, how would I pull that off? I had spiralled into such a destructive lifestyle I wouldn't even know where to begin. Oh my god, I wasn't going to be able to. I'd go right back to using! Shit shit shit....

I began looking around nervously at everyone, I reached up and rubbed my forehead with my hands, hiding my face, squinting my eyes shut shaking my head back and forth. I was doomed, I might as well just go upstairs and rig that sheet up into a nice rope and hang myself. I glanced over at the door desperately. I needed to get out of there, and fast. I jumped up and strolled towards the door, not looking back.

"Cass! Come sit down!" Ordered Carol with an extremely authoritative voice. I froze, glancing back at her. Looking forlorn and scared, I shook my head slowly. She got up, walked to me without breaking eye contact, and escorted me back to my seat.

"Sit down Cass. You will stay. You will participate. You will be sad. And sad won't kill you. So just be here, be sad, and notice how you're still alive."

I burst into tears again, holding my face in my hands, rocking back and forth in my chair. I felt a warm hand rubbing my back, telling me it was going to get better, just hang in there and I would see. I don't think I heard much of the topic that day. But I stayed. And I was sad. And it didn't kill me...and the fact that I could just be with my feelings and they wouldn't kill me was a bigger lesson than any other I could have learned that day.

We had group every day in the afternoon. Each day it was the same, always starting with the same introductions, and I noticed the impact of adding one more day to my number of days clean. I was actually beginning to feel proud of myself. Every now and then a new girl would arrive. She would cry, look scared, and usually try to leave. I was so far past that now. I actually joined the conversations, asked some questions, added some opinions. I even laughed now and then. I was beginning to get that these people cared about me. I came to realize that Jenny was one of the sweetest kindest people I had ever known. She actually reminded me a lot of Lili. One day I told group about Lili. I told them how it had ripped my heart out. How I had wanted to die. How using was the only way I knew of coping with these feelings. I slowly began to learn new ways of dealing with feelings. Each day I grew emotionally stronger and more capable. I was actually beginning to see how life on the outside might even be possible.

I knew they had an outpatient program. I wanted to talk to Alex about whether or not I should join this when I was finished here. It turns out she was already a step ahead of me, and when she visited me on a Friday afternoon, she told me she had already set it all up for me. She said I would not be going straight back to my apartment but would be living in a half-way house for a while, getting ongoing treatment, and slowly transitioning back into normal life as a non-user. In the meantime, she was looking after things at my apartment as necessary and keeping my family members informed. She was being a true friend, and I know I could never have done any of this without her.

Chapter 33

The Routine

Eventually I settled into the routine. We got up, showered and got ready for the day, ate breakfast communally, tidied up our space, headed to craft or activity, ate lunch, went to group, rested, went to dinner, then socialized in the common areas. This usually consisted of TV, card games, lively chats, and general girl bonding. Not that there weren't fights. There were, and some terrible ones.

One evening after supper I had been sitting on a couch half watching TV and chatting with a few girls when one of the newer girls began throwing a fit, yelling at Jenny because Jenny had sat in her seat. Jenny refused to move, letting her know that all vacant seats were open to anyone who wished to sit in them. The other girl stood tall over Jenny, hands on her hips, yelling at her, calling her a cunt, a bitch, a fucking whore even. I couldn't take it, I stood up, took a swift punch at the girl, and dropped her instantly. Apparently, this was not allowed. Shit. As they were escorting me off to some kind of detention, I heard Jenny whisper "Thank you Cass, thank you for defending me, I love you girl".

I got taken to a small office with myself, three administrators and a note-taker present for the meeting. I was scared they were going to throw me out. I remember vaguely being told about the no-violence policy, but I really never dreamed it would apply to me.

"So, can you tell us what happened in there Cassandra?

Oh...sorry, I'm Vanessa, I'm in charge of disciplinary action around here."

"Uh...." I began, "I don't know. I punched her. She was coming down on Jenny, threatening her, calling her names, I just pounced, I reacted. I was defending Jenny. She had no right to be intimidating her like that. Jenny's a sweet girl, she didn't deserve that. I was protecting her. And that's it."

"Are you aware of the no-violence policy here Cass?" Vanessa stared at me in a stern but hopeful way, almost willing me to not fail this interview.

"Yeah, I remember being briefed when I first got here." I hung my head in shame, I was beginning to feel a bit hopeless.

"And you've seen the posters that are in the hallways, the dorm rooms, and the cafeteria reminding you of the house rules?"

"Yeah, I suppose I've seen those too." I was feeling worse and worse, and I looked down so they wouldn't see my tears. *Please don't kick me out* I prayed silently. I had been here for 20 days and I had over a full week left. I knew I was much better, but I wasn't ready for the outside.

They asked me a few more questions, then left the room to deliberate for a while, leaving just myself and the note-taker who had been quietly documenting the meeting. After ten minutes of leaving me to sweat, the three ladies came back in, and Vanessa spoke:

"Cassandra, we are going to need some time to come to a decision. Right now, we are divided on whether or not to allow you to stay. You will spend some time in the Quiet Thinking Space. We will let you know when we've made our decision. I was led down a few hallways, around a few corners, through a few doors, and then buzzed into the area of the facility that I had started in. They led me down a corridor that I recognized from my first few weeks in detox. I walked past my old room. No one was in it at the moment.

I stopped and stared in for a few seconds. I was having flashbacks of the cold sweats, the constant throwing up, the fevers, and chills, and the pure hell that I had gone through in that room. It seemed like a thousand days ago already. It was so hard to believe that was only three weeks ago. They prompted me to keep walking, but I looked back as I moved forward. I had the creeps, as though the ghost of me was still lurking in that room. I shook it off and kept going.

We arrived at my new quarters. I had a bed, a private bathroom, and was promised breakfast in the morning. They told me to settle in for the night, that I would be sleeping here, and that some time tomorrow they should have their answer. It was going to be a long night. It was only 9 pm, and I wasn't yet tired, and there was nothing here but me and my thoughts. They locked the door behind me and showed me the intercom I could use if I had any questions or concerns, but that they were hoping not to hear from me.

I laid on my back on the bed. Fuck them. I didn't need them. I was fine. I could leave here and be just fine. In fact, I might even be glad to get out of here, I could finally get that fix I'd been dreaming about. I didn't know what else to do, and I was waffling back and forth between false bravado and pure anxiety, so I undressed and began to fantasize about having sex. Since I had had mostly shitty experiences with men, my mind wandered to the amazing experience I'd had with Alex so long ago. Eventually my imagination settled on Jenny. I pictured her caring for me, rubbing my back, brushing the hair off of my forehead, and then suddenly leaning over and kissing me. I slipped my hand under the covers and began brushing my fingertips lightly over my pussy as I imagined Jenny pressing her tongue into my mouth and me moaning. I pictured reaching up and cupping her breast while she continued kissing me passionately. My fingers probed further into my rapidly swelling pussy, and I found that I was dripping wet. I dipped my fingers into my wetness and began circling my clit with my fingers. I imagined undoing Jenny's blouse, peeling it off of her, reaching around her to undo her bra, and seeing her naked breasts for the first time. I imagined popping one of them into my mouth and sucking her nipple until she moaned. I felt the mounting urge to come, and I pictured peeling off her pants and panties, and lunging for her pussy with my mouth. As I imagined what she tasted like, I began to climax, thrusting my hips up to my hand, moaning out loud, and finishing myself off with a satisfied sigh.

I feel asleep naked and with my wet hand resting on my pussy, which was slightly awkward when the attendant arrived with breakfast the next morning. The good news was I was informed that in an hour the decision makers would be meeting with me to advise me of my fate.

Chapter 34

Life was Good

D ave and I lounged about in bed for a few more hours, playfully cuddling, kissing, tickling each other's backs, lovingly caressing each other. It was beautiful. It was fulfilling. It was everything I had fought this hard to get to. Life had certainly not been easy over the past few years. I had climbed a long hard road up from nothing and now I had everything. I was enjoying marvelling in the amazingness of it all.

We eventually got up and made a pot of coffee and sat around his kitchen island chatting. He in pyjama bottoms, me in his dress shirt. He made me eggs, and we devoured them like we hadn't eaten in weeks. I couldn't think of a better way to start our day and our lives together. Dave knew what I had been through and he still loved me. He knew about the prostitution years; he knew about the drug abuse. He knew about the rehab; he knew about the death of Lili. He even knew about my experimenting with women. And he loved me. He loved me in spite of it all. Or maybe he loved me because of it all. All I knew was that I was never going to let him go again. I promised him that if fears or concerns came up, I would talk to him instead of running from him. We held hands, we goofily stared into each other's eyes, grinning like teenagers in love. We had the most amazing day of my life.

Chapter 35

Getting Sorted Out

I got up and had a quick shower, bashfully remembering the fantasy that I had fallen asleep to the night before. I thought about touching myself in the shower, and grazed my hand lightly over my pubic hair, but then worried I wouldn't be done before the decision-makers arrived. I soaped up my breasts, squeezing my nipples slightly, giving myself a small shudder and wishing I had a way to relieve my tension. I stepped out, dried off, and nervously pulled a quick brush through my hair and brushed my teeth with the basic supplies they had left me in the bathroom. After dressing, I sat on my bed chewing my nails nervously waiting for my fate to be delivered. It had become very clear to me that I was not ready to leave. I had nothing else right now except this place. It had literally saved my life. I was not ready to leave.

"Cassandra." Vanessa addressed me as the three ladies walked through the door. "I trust you slept well and found the supplies you needed in the bathroom." This was a statement more than a question. Nonetheless I nodded anxiously.

"Yes fine, just fine" I brushed it off, awaiting the much more pressing topic at hand.

"We've just come from a meeting. We met with the director of the facility, our lawyer, and your social worker. We also asked Alex to come in. We are concerned for your well-being, Cassandra, but we are also concerned for the well-being of the other patients." All I could do was nod at this point, petrified. I was sitting up straight with my fingernails between my teeth as though ready to bite, the other hand draped across my stomach, as though it could calm my nerves down.

"We've considered what the risk is of you staying. With this violent outburst, we are concerned that it will happen again. Especially considering that Elsa, the woman you assaulted, is still a patient at our facility, and you two would have to co-exist for another week if we let you stay to *completion*." Completion was the state of having completed the entire program as intended, attended all of the group sessions, the individual sessions, and passed the interview with the discharging doctor.

"Oh, I see" I mumbled, mostly defeated. "So, this is it then?"

"Well, perhaps we have come up with a way for you to stay". This got my attention. I wanted, no needed to stay. At this point they had me for whatever they wanted me for. I would have bent over and taken it up the ass right then and there if I thought it would have helped.

"After consulting with the various members of our meeting, we have come up with a strategy that has satisfied all in attendance which would allow you to stay".

"Go on" I breathed; my eyes glued to Vanessa.

"You will have to begin by having a meeting with Elsie, during which some of us will be present to facilitate. During this meeting, you will come to understand each other's viewpoints, perspectives, thought, feelings, and wishes around what happened, and what will happen going forward. You will sincerely apologize to her during this meeting, and she must agree to have you stay. Second, if all goes well with that meeting, you will issue a statement to the rest of the patients, in writing, that you will read out loud to them. You will discuss what you did, why you think it was unacceptable, that you accept the consequence of legal action and expulsion from the facility if it should happen again and will explain to them what your consequence will be after you are discharged. Which brings us to the third point. You will be required to do 300 hours of community service after you are discharged, and failure to complete this within 60 days will result in legal disciplinary action, meaning you could go to jail. So....Cassandra....do you agree to these terms?"

"Yes, yes, thank you, I agree to all of it." I don't even think I was letting any of it sink it, I just felt that it was some sort of lifeline being sent to me, so I grabbed on for dear life. I took a deep breath and asked when I could get started.

Chapter 36

Retribution

I was led straight from that meeting to another meeting room back in the main wing where I had spent the past several weeks. I was asked to wait there, so I got to sit and stare at the note-taking woman for another ten to fifteen minutes of awkward silence. When the group re-entered the room, Elsie was now with them. The only ones that stayed in the room were me, the note-taker, Vanessa, and Elsie. The others excused themselves (presumably to watch from behind the obvious two-way mirror to our left).

"Ok, I think we all know why we are here today. Cassandra, do you have any questions before we start?"

"Um....no, I don't think so" I mumbled, shaking my head.

"Good, good. Well then, Elsie, how about you, do you have any questions as to why you are here, or what is going to happen here?" followed Vanessa.

"Nope, I aint got no questions, fire this meeting up!" Elsie's eyes danced as she spoke, almost daring me to try to win her over. And I could tell she wasn't going to be an easy sell.

"Excellent. Well then, let's begin" Vanessa went on. "Cassandra, you may start. Please explain what was going on for you when you assaulted Elsie".

Um....ok. Well, Elsie, I felt that you were being a horrible terrible bitch and you were wrong to bully Jenny. I thought you were a jerk, and that's why I punched you". I could see Vanessa cringing and slowly shaking her head while watching in horror as these words tumbled out of my mouth. But I pressed on anyhow, "And furthermore, I probably would have punched you again if given half a chance". By now I could see Elsie starting to fume. Her fists were clenched, her jaw became clenched. She basically looked ready to punch me. She tried to interject, but Vanessa stopped her, telling her I was allowed to finish.

"Do you have more, Cassandra?"

"Yes, I have more, I just need to gather my thoughts". I sat pondering for a few minutes. I really wanted to get this right. I took a deep breath and pushed on.

"I care about Jenny. I mean I *really* care about Jenny. I had a friend named Lili who died of suicide after an overdose. She struggled with drugs and it was my fault. I let her get involved in my terrible lifestyle. I let her get hurt. I let her die. This hangs over me, and this is what ultimately led me to my drug addiction, which eventually landed me in here. I was angry. At Lili, at the people that hurt her, at her death, pretty much at the whole world for my shitty life. When I saw you standing over Jenny, scaring her and threatening her well-being, I just lost it for a moment. For one moment you represented everything bad that ever happened to Lili and all the people that hurt her. You represented her being ripped away from me. And you weren't going to take Jenny away from me now. I have grown to love her and feel protective of her like I did with Lili, but this time I didn't want to screw it up. I see now that she didn't need protecting. You were not threatening her life. You were not threatening to take her away from me. You were just yelling at her. I feel silly now that I see the difference. Elsie, I overreacted. I blamed you for all of my pain, and I just wanted to punch it away. I'm so sorry." I paused here, tearing up.

"Elsie, can you forgive me? You seem like a decent person who's just struggling with your own set of demons – not unlike the rest of us. You deserve respect and fair treatment, and I didn't give you that. I'm sorry. You have my word I will not take my own shit out on you, or anyone else here again". I paused again, looking into her eyes with an open mind and an open heart to whatever she wished to share back with me. She looked softened for a minute. She even almost teared up. Then she snapped back to coldness and blurted out,

"Yeah, well sorry doesn't cut it bitch. You can't just go around punching people. I don't forgive you; I hope you rot in hell! I want out of here, let me out, I'm done!" and with that, she strode to the door and started yanking on the knob. "Let me out you goons, I'm done in here!" she kept shaking the knob until someone came and let her out and led her back to her quarters. I just sat and sobbed. I had tried my best. I had failed. I was defeated. They escorted me back to my regular quarters and asked me to wait there until I was notified. I waited there for the better part of three hours before I heard anything. I spent the time dreaming up ways I was going to succeed on the outside. I didn't have a plan yet, but I had started working on a plan with my counsellor this week, and I knew Alex was arranging after-care at a half-way house of some sort. I was beginning to believe that maybe I would be ok. I could do this, right? I mean, I had overcome loads of tough shit in my past. I could handle getting kicked out of rehab a week early. I laid down on my back, closed my eyes, and began daydreaming about how I would make it on the outside. I woke up a few hours later.

"Cass, Cass, wake up." I was startled awake to find Jenny excitedly shaking my shoulder.

"Jenny? What are you doing here? I....I thought I was still being quarantined while they got ready to evict me".

"No silly, they sent me in to give you the good news". She was positively beaming. I noticed when I looked up at her that the way the light shone behind her head gave her a magical glow. She was smiling so sweetly, I got lost in the moment thinking that she was my angel. In that moment, something in me began to heal. I began to let Lili go, realizing Jenny had been put in my life to let me love and trust again. I just grabbed her and yanked her in close, squeezing, and not letting go.

"Jenny, I love you so much. You have no idea. You're my angel. Thank you for believing in me, thank you for loving me." She chuckled and pulled away,

"Easy Cass" she chuckled, "I'm not going anywhere!" She just smiled at me. "And, incidentally, neither are you!".

Chapter 37

Exit Strategy

My last week in rehab consisted of meetings with my group, meetings with my individual counsellor, meetings with my exit counsellor, and group meetings with all of my counsellors, Alex, and my sister Janice. We were preparing me for the real world...building an exit strategy if you will. A halfway house had been selected, and I would be moving straight there from here. I would have to spend my first few months fulfilling my community service work, which should serve to keep me busy and out of trouble while I transitioned. Alex had been looking after my apartment, and she and Janice had gone and picked out a bunch of my clothes and personal items that I would take to the halfway house with me. Alex would keep my keys and I was strictly forbidden from going back there yet. She would have to be my liaison if I needed anything. I also had the chance to read my apology letter to the group, which was both powerful and humbling. Afterwards, Jenny came up to me and told me my letter was beautiful and inspiring. I told her that I thought she was beautiful and inspiring.

I spent every spare moment with Jenny. She and I had grown very close, and I often thought about kissing her soft silky lips, holding her close to me, caressing her hair, undressing her, making love to her with my mouth and hands. I thought about a lot of stuff, but I hadn't made any sort of move on her. Jenny was due to leave shortly after me – she had been on a longer program than I was. This was not her first time in, and she had both drug and alcohol addictions, and had been on suicide watch for a while. She was doing so well now though. I believed this time would be different for her, that she would really make something of herself and her life this time. She was scheduled to be entering a different halfway house than I was, but only about 30 minutes away by bus, so we planned to spend our spare time together on the outside.

My outside training consisted of preparing me with activities to fill my days, a host of ways to decline invitations from bad influence acquaintances, how to get through social events where there was access to drugs and/or alcohol, and all of the relationship building skills we had been learning all month. We had also spent a considerable amount of time learning to deal with our emotions appropriately. Basically, I had learned to use my big girl words. Even with all this training though, I was scared shitless. The night before I was due to leave, I started hyperventilating in the TV room where Jenny and I had been watching TV alone. Jenny ran and got me water and sat with me, comforting me, telling me everything was going to be ok. She held me and rocked me, kissing me on the forehead, holding my face in her hands. I looked up at her and swiped at my eyes.

"Is it really going to be ok Jenny?"

"Yeah, it really is baby, you're going to be just fine on the outside. We're going to hang out lots, we'll get real jobs, go back to living on our own...maybe we'll even get a place together! I think life is going to be amazing. I think you're amazing." I suddenly reached up and pulled her face to mine and kissed her hungrily on the lips. I pushed my tongue inside her mouth – she didn't pull away. She kissed me back, awkwardly at first, then with fervour. We kissed as though our lives depended on this connection. She allowed me to reach inside her blouse and squeeze her breasts; she let out a moan, which whipped me into a more heightened state,

"Oh Jenny, I want you so bad – I hope you know I'm completely in love with you, I would do anything for you, you're my angel". And with that, she pulled back gently, stood up, and took me by the hand. You need to get some sleep; you have a big day tomorrow". She led me back to our room, put me to bed, and crawled in behind me, spooning me until I fell asleep. When I woke up, she wasn't there, and I got woken up with a bunch of flurry and commotion, as they excitedly told me my ride is here, I need to grab my stuff, I need to go!! I looked around for Jenny, but couldn't find her, and they kept sweeping me up in the commotion, so I figured I'd see her on my way out. I kept looking and asking, but I never ran into her. I ran up to greet Alex, who swept me up with a gigantic hug and she told me she had already signed all the paperwork and we should be off, as I had an early check-in at Cedar Crescent Halfway House. I asked one of the other girls to tell Jenny I would catch up with her – I knew the name of her home and would come by on the weekend. I was sad to have missed her, but excited about my new journey! Outside world – here I come!

Chapter 38

Moving into a Relationship

Things with Dave were perfect. I began spending weekends at his place. We would make love at night, lounge around in the mornings, eat a leisurely breakfast, drink some coffee, then eventually wander off to town to run errands, or head out for some exercise. I was feeling fitter and healthier than ever. We usually cooked at home, we began working out together in his small home gym, and we would often go for a hike in the hills, or a jog around his neighbourhood. I was leaving to go home on a Sunday night so that I would have clothes for work on Monday morning when Dave hugged me, breathed into my hair, and mumbled,

"I wish you didn't have to go...why don't you have more stuff here?"

"Yeah, that would be nice...it's not even too long of a drive to work from here if I take the freeway all the way in....."

"Hmmmm, well maybe you should consider bringing more of your stuff here" he drew my face up to look him in the eyes. I moved in three days later. I mean, I kept my apartment, but I never stayed there. We went over two or three times to collect clothes and personal items; he cleared out space in the dresser and closet for me and kept asking if I wanted to bring any of my furniture or decorations over. I really didn't care about any of that. My apartment had long lost its appeal to me, since it carried so many terrible memories of the woman that I no longer was. For the time, I basically abandoned the place and went back only when I was looking for something I'd forgotten to bring.

Dave and I fell into a nice routine. We'd get up together, get ready for work, leave around the same time, and meet back after work to cook dinner, hang out in the evenings, and then go to bed, tucked neatly into each other's arms, all safe, warm, and loved. I couldn't ask for more, and I truly believed I had everything I could possibly want. I wouldn't change a thing. Not on purpose anyways.

Chapter 39

Cedar Crescent

I hopped into Alex's car after giving Janice a kiss goodbye and confirming when she was coming to the halfway house to visit me. I was eager. I felt fresh. I was starting to really believe I could do this. I didn't have much of a plan yet as far as what I was going to do with my life after my community service was complete, and once I was able to move out of the half-way house and back on my own. I would need a proper job, a proper support system, and to begin to rebuild all aspects of my life. I knew I didn't have to figure it all out now, though; I just needed to get from one day to the next while sober for now. The rest I would figure out over the new several months from the safety of Cedar Crescent.

We pulled up to the front of Cedar Crescent and I was surprised at how unimpressive it was. For some reason I was expecting something fancy or stately or modern. It was none of those things. It was a smallish house on a main street of a quiet neighbourhood. There were other houses down the street, but it was on a corner, and there was a park to one side and an empty lot on the other. There was a bus stop outside, which I was glad about, and I suppose it seemed serene. And I could hardly imagine getting into much trouble around here. We walked up the steps and Alex knocked. We were greeted by Molly, one of the "house moms". She was a large stately woman with her hair all up in a head scarf with big hoop earrings. I was mesmerized by the large gap between her two front teeth and how she smelled of lilacs. I remember following her inside the house briefly wondering if we would call her Mom, or Molly. Turns out we were to call her Molly. But inside my head, I often called her Mom secretly. She was everything I had ever wished my mom to be.... commanding, kind, self-assured, forgiving, and stern, all rolled into one loud and impressive woman who never left you wondering how she felt. And right from the beginning I felt her love for all of the women in the house, myself included. I was feeling like life was really going to come together for me. Cedar Crescent had me feeling safe and confident from the beginning.

I was shown to my room, which I would share with one other woman. There were two single beds, 2 dressers, and a small window overlooking the park. We were allowed to put up any decorations, photos, knick-knacks etc. none of which I had with me anyhow. Maybe eventually I'd send Alex to pick up a photo or two, so I felt more at home. My roommate Sarah was currently not home. She was employed full time at the local grocery store and was due home by dinner. Alex hung out for a bit, but then let me know it was time for her to go so Molly could get me properly settled and acquainted with the house and the house rules. It was tough to say goodbye to Alex, but I knew I'd see her again in a few days. I put on a brave face and waved at her from the doorway. Then I turned back, gently closed the door, and began my new life.

There was a total of 10 residents, including myself. In this particular home, we had our food provided and dinners prepared for us, we had shared laundry facilities, which we took care of ourselves, and we had expected chore lists. I met a few of the residents, but most were gone to work or school. I knew I had today to settle in, but then I would have to start my community services tomorrow. Molly and I sat down to have a proper meeting, where she explained everything that was expected of me. There was zero tolerance for not maintaining sobriety. That was the main rule. Also, there was a 10 pm curfew, and all guests had to be gone by 9 pm. We all had to clean up after ourselves and would be assigned house chores at the beginning of each week. If we failed to follow the rules, this could result in a loss of privileges, a fine, or even expulsion. I was given a time slot in which to do laundry – 5-9 pm on Wednesdays. I was issued a monthly bus pass and given a bus schedule, and it was explained to me that I could add cooking duties if I wanted to reduce my monthly fee or receive some extra money. I decided that I should take on cooking duties ASAP, since I had no source of income, and it might be nice to be able to buy a snack, or the odd meal out, or even take a taxi now and then while I was fulfilling my community services.

The day ended up flying by. Sarah and many of the others were home around 5:30 or 6, and we ate dinner at 7 pm. Slowly, I began to get to know the girls. They seemed like a pretty chill group for the most part. I really saw myself fitting in here well. Sarah was quiet and had a kind face. She welcomed me and told me to let her know if I needed anything. I was nervous to be too optimistic, but so far things seemed really great here. I ended up crashing around 10 pm, as I was tired from the excitement, and knew I had a full day ahead of me tomorrow. I had been briefed on where I needed to show up in the morning, had my bus pass tucked into my pocket, and felt ready to take on the next day, and the next chapter of my life. I drifted off to sleep thinking about Jenny and looking forward to seeing her soon. However, I tossed and turned, and had terrible dreams about monsters chasing me, corpses falling to the ground in front of me, and being stuck in glue when I tried to run. In my dream I tried to scream, but all that would come out was a squeak. I woke up in the middle of the night in a cold sweat with Molly perched on the bed beside me, stroking my hair, telling me everything was going to be ok, that I was safe, and it was just a bad dream. Hmm, just like a mom. With that thought I thanked her, turned over, smiled, and went back to sleep, instead dreaming of being a child with my mom pushing me on a swing in the sunshine. I felt safe.

Chapter 40

Community Service

I got up at 7:00 AM, made a quick coffee and toast, grabbed my bagged lunch, and waved goodbye to Molly, who wished me well. I was out at the bus stop at 7:25 waiting for the 7:30 bus, anxiously glancing up the street praying I hadn't missed the bus. I was dressed in a modest skirt and blouse with 2-inch heels and my hair pulled back into a sleek ponytail. I looked good. Molly had helped me pick out my outfit and told me I looked great – very professional. At least I hoped so. Alex had arranged that I would fulfill my community service at the courthouse. I would be filing, organizing, note-taking, shredding, and photocopying for the offices of the district attorney. I was extremely lucky to have landed such a great gig, and I did not take this for granted. I showed up 15 minutes early and reported to Margaret, the administrative assistant. She put me to work immediately. I was set to put in 8-hour days, 5 days a week for approximately 2 months, but could be done in a little as 7 ½ weeks if I didn't miss any work.

At first Margaret seemed stern and unfriendly. I did my best to action everything she asked of me. I wanted her to like me, even to think I was doing a good job. It ended up being a hard day on my feet all day, but at 4:30, when Margaret tapped me on the shoulder and told me it was time to go home, I was surprised at how quickly the time had passed. She smiled warmly at me for the first time and told me I had done a really good job today and that she looked forward to seeing me tomorrow. I was beaming all the way home on the bus. Look at me, an honest working office girl once again. It seemed like so long ago that I had had a respectable job. I could really get used to this. I wondered how Jenny was getting along. I couldn't wait to call her next week when she got to her halfway house to see if her transition went as well as mine was going.

Day two at the office. Same tasks, but she also asked me to run some errands. I dropped papers off to other offices, picked up supplies from the storage room, and even got to pick up coffee for a meeting. I couldn't have been happier. Things at the home were smooth as well. Sarah was easy to get along with, Molly was warm and encouraging, Martha, the cook, was funny, and one hell of a cook. I started helping her in the kitchen after a few days. She had me chopping, dicing, prepping, stirring and mixing. I didn't mind. The more I had to do the less I thought about getting high or feeling depressed. I would get home from work by 5:30 every day and get changed into sweats and a t-shirt, and immediately head to the kitchen to help Martha. She gave me more and more responsibilities and I was learning a lot from her. I could braise a chicken, cook a roast, sauté vegetables, and create delicious sauces. I was beginning to fancy myself as somewhat of a cook. Hmmm, maybe one day I would actually consider a life of settling down with a man and becoming somewhat domestic even!

By the second week at work, Margaret pretty much trusted me with everything. She had me setting up meetings, delivering documents, calling for appointments, and assisting with serving snacks at the meetings. I would show the guests in, serve coffee, fetch notepads or pens, and mostly just smile. It was usually businesspeople, lawyers, and executive types. I never knew what the meetings were about, I was gone with the door shut by the time they started. It didn't get past me, however, that there were a lot of handsome successful looking men in those rooms. Sometimes they would flirt with me a little with a smile, and warm thank you, or a nice comment. I would demurely smile back and thank them politely before blushing and turning away. I loved the attention, but these men DID NOT want to get involved with me. I was not their type. Their type was either the businesswomen, or the "Suzy Homemaker" type. If only they knew the real me. They would run the other direction as fast as they could. And rightfully so; I didn't deserve guys like these. Hell, I'm not sure I even believed I deserved to be loved at all.

Chapter 41

Where's Jenny?

I made it through the week happy and exhausted. I knew Jenny was getting out Friday, and that I would be able to call her Saturday. I was excited to talk to her and find out all about her new home and her new life. I woke up at 7, had breakfast, did my Saturday chores quickly, then signed up for phone time at 10 am for 30 minutes. I was so excited I shook as I dialled her number. It rang three times and a woman answered,

"Hello, Marjorie here, how can I help you?".

"Uh, hi Marjorie, this is Cassandra from Cedar Crescent....and, um, I'd like to speak to Jenny, she's new there, she just arrived last night I believe....is she there, can I speak to her? I gushed.

There was a long silence on the other end of the phone. The woman seemed confused, she stammered,
"Oh, uh...Jenny's not here. I mean, I don't know...uh...well, I'm not sure. Hold on." The line was silent for a minute.

"Hello, you're looking for Jenny?" Asked a new voice.

"Yes, Jenny, she should have arrived last night." More silence. Then just,
"I'm sorry, there's no Jenny here." And the phone went click.

I hung the phone up confused. I tried to call Alex, but she

didn't pick up, so I left her a message asking her to find out where Jenny was. I called the rehab centre, but they couldn't give out patient information. So, I was left all weekend wondering what had become of her. Maybe she had changed homes at the last minute and would contact me when she could. Or maybe they wanted her to stay a little longer at the rehab centre. It was driving me crazy not knowing. I was chewing the end of my pen pondering this when Sarah came in.

"Hey Cass, what's up? You look worried."

"I was expecting my friend Jenny to get out of rehab yesterday and now I can't find her at the half-way house she was supposed to be going to. I'm just a little worried." A frown crept over my face. Seeing this, Sarah quickly replied,

"Well, it could be anything, I wouldn't worry, give it a few days and you'll probably hear from her. In the meantime, I'm going shopping down at the village if you'd care to join – I need a new pair of shoes for work and I hear there's a great sale on at the discount shoe store." Sarah and I grabbed our bus passes and spent a nice afternoon shoe shopping, picking up a few things Sarah needed, and afterwards she treated me to lunch at a cafe. It was really good to be out just doing normal things like errands, shopping, and socializing. I was able to forget about worrying over Jenny's whereabouts for a while, and was beginning to think it probably was nothing, just a last-minute change of plans. I would hear from her soon.

We were headed back towards the bus stop when I thought I saw Jenny on the street. It was a woman who looked like a junkie running by screaming random words. Her head was turned so I couldn't really see her face. It wasn't Jenny. Of course, it couldn't be – Jenny wasn't a junkie. She was a sweet girl who was on her way to making something of her life. I shook my head. I really needed to get her off my mind for a while. Of course she wasn't running by, shouting obscenities like a lunatic. I chuckled. Then

I realized that that had been me at one time. And probably Jenny, and probably Sarah. And all of the intakes at the rehab centre and all of the residents at Cedar Crescent. That's when it really hit me. I had been that woman. I had been destined for hard cold street life, loss of all friends, family, dignity, and health, and certain death. And now look where I was. I sat down on the curb side and put my head in my hands and just began to sob. I sobbed and sobbed, tears streaking down my face, my head shaking back and forth. I tried to get the words out when Sarah sat beside me, but she just nodded and said, "I know". She did know. And in that moment, I knew beyond a shadow of a doubt that I would never ever take drugs again. I would never sell my body again. I would never again be in pursuit of the ultimate control in the act of dominating another human, and I would never be in the pursuit of the total loss of control while achieving my next high. For now, for once, I could just be. Sarah held me for a while, and eventually we stood up, and without talking about what had happened, we walked over to the bus, got on, rode home, and continued moving forward.

Chapter 42

Damn You Addiction

Three days later I found out where Jenny was. Jenny was dead. She had been released on Friday as planned, but she never made it to the half-way house. Instead, she headed directly to the streets, got herself high, got herself more high, then got herself high enough to be dead. I'll never know if it was Jenny that I saw on the street that day, but I suspected it might have been. When I heard the news, Sarah and Molly (our house mom) were with me. I crumpled to the floor sobbing and wailing. Both women sat down on the floor with me and just held me. We sat like that rocking, with them stroking my hair and my back, brushing the hair from my face, wiping my tears, holding me tight. I held to those two women like my life depended on it. And it did. Somehow, they eventually got me to my bed and tucked me under the covers. One of them sat with me for the rest of the day, reading to me, watching me sleep, bringing me water and snacks that I would mostly push away. If I went to the bathroom, they waited on the other side of the door and talked to me until I came out. I know that they took turns staying awake watching me overnight. I didn't mind and I didn't blame them. I could easily have walked out that front door, found myself high, and either overdosed, or been sucked completely and eternally back into that world. It was so close. It probably would have happened had they left me alone for 5 minutes. As many of them that could gathered around me as often as possible. It was annoying, but completely necessary. They talked to me about nothing, mundane life stuff. They bitched about bosses, complained about the cost of haircuts, and told me about cute guys they had met. I didn't care about any of it. But somehow it got me through the worst of it. This kept on for nearly a week. Molly had called my boss and I had a full week before I was due back. Even with the week off, I could still achieve my mandated hours by my required end date, as long as I didn't take off any sick days before then.

On day four I joined the others at the dinner table and my round-the-clock supervision had been scaled back. I later found out that I was on what they called code blue. Since I had experienced a huge emotional trauma and I was so early on in my recovery, I was considered at high risk of suicide and/or re-lapse. I later had the privilege of supervising other girls through their own code blues, and I never forgot how this group got me through mine. I learned a lot that week. I learned that terrible sorrow could be felt without killing me. I learned that people loved me and would always be there for me. I learned how important my recovery group was to my long-term wellbeing. I learned that I could get through life without using. I was attending group again by day 4 as well. Anyone in the house at 8:30 pm took part in group to debrief about their day, share insights, and have a place to feel supported. That day my group just gathered around me and hugged me for the first 10 minutes. We then slowly made our way to our seats, and the others took turns sharing whatever was on their minds. When everyone had spoken, Molly turned to me and asked me to share with the group how I was feeling. I took a deep breath and faced the group.

"First of all," I began through tears, "Thank you guys. Thank you for saving my life." I began to sob, but just kept looking around the room with tears streaming down my face. "Without you guys I would be back on the streets, or possibly dead as well." I couldn't save Jenny, but you all saved me." I took a moment to cry for my loss. Gently, Molly asked me to please share anything else I was feeling.

"I feel so damn fucking guilty. I feel like I could have saved her. I feel like I let Jenny down. I feel like it's my fault somehow." By now I was hick-upping and speaking through sobs.

"I feel like it's not fair. I am so fucking mad at her for doing this! Why did she do this? Why?" I looked around the room as though one of them could tell me, staring at them through tear-stained eyes, begging someone to explain this to me.

"I know Cass, I know. It's so tragic and terrible, and such a waste and it sucks, and it's fucked up, and it's not fair. All of that is true" said Molly, nodding her head in understanding. Addiction is cruel, addiction is merciless. It takes too many of us". We all held hands in our little circle then and looked at each other through our own tears and vowed then and there to always save each other, to always be there for each other, and to always love each other. We would survive. We had each other. I went back to work on Monday and allowed myself to move forward and begin to heal. I was ready to move forward, and my work at the courthouse felt like my new life, my new direction, my hope for my future. I didn't realize at the time just how true this was, but my life was about to change big time.

Chapter 43

Men

As part of recovery, we were encouraged to refrain from romantic relationships for a year. I believed this on some level, but the girls in recovery were constantly ignoring this rule. Some had notably replaced using with fucking. Others just craved constant attention from men to attempt to hold up their flailing self-esteem. Most addicts have a story, and many of the stories go something like I felt unloved or mistreated growing up. Most addicts aren't nearly aware of this though. So, dating (though frowned upon) was rampant in Cedar Crescent. I tended to believe that I was not ready to date. Plus, I was a bit confused as to which way I would go once I started dating. I was attracted to men sexually, though I was mixed up sexually as to what I wanted or liked. Women held a certain appeal to me too; however, it was more in a nurturing, safe way. I was probably not a lesbian, just someone who sought comfort in female relationships, and was so messed up sexually that I didn't know when it should enter into a romantic relationship and when it shouldn't. I decided that when I was ready to start dating, I would be focussing on men as my target audience. But for now, I was happy to wait out my year.

Work was going really well. I was in my final week and had been putting out resumes every day after work looking for something that I could transition into when my volunteer hours were complete. Margaret was such a pleasure to work for. She encouraged me, assured me I was doing a great job, gave me tips and advice to improve my work ethic, and told me she'd keep an eye out for anyone hiring and be sure to put in a good word for me if she was asked.

I was sitting on a bench in one of the hallways during a break Monday morning and a handsome man sat on the bench next to me. He appeared to be around 35, looked well-off, and carried himself with certain authority. I glanced at him sideways to catch him staring at me.

"Hiya" he ventured first.

"Hey" I countered before quickly glancing back down at my lap. Shit, this guy was cute! He stared me down for a moment, then slid down the bench until he was sitting directly beside me. I felt a bit uncomfortable, as he was awkwardly close, but I smiled up at him shyly and then glanced back down at my hands resting on my lap. He reached over and patted my hand gently.

"Hi, I'm Peter. And I happen to think you are wildly sexy." I wasn't quite sure what to make of this, I frowned a bit, bit my lip and wondered if I was over-reacting to a simple friendly gesture and compliment. Then Peter continued,

"I know who you are. You're Cassandra, aren't you?" I nodded slowly, looking at him sceptically out of the corner of my eye.

"Don't worry Cassandra, I know who you are, but your secret's safe with me." He raised him eyebrows knowingly and teased his tongue across his teeth for effect. He slid his hand onto my leg and began to slide it up my skirt slowly, staring at me with a wicked grin on his face. I pushed his hand away and slid down the bench, trying not to cause any scene.

"Oh, is that how you play? A little cat and mouse game? Hmm, I like the idea of a chase". I immediately got up and fled down the hall as fast as I could, not looking back. I paused once I got into the offices I worked in and breathed a sigh of relief, leaning back against the closed door.

"Whatever is the matter, Cassandra?" asked Margaret frowning and peering at me closely over her glasses.

"Oh, it's nothing, I just thought I was late, so I rushed in." I rushed off to work on files while feeling her gaze follow me inquisitively. She didn't need to think that I was causing any trouble by being here. Especially when I was so close to being done, and with no bad reports on my record so far, I wanted to keep it that way.

Wednesday afternoon I needed some supplies, so I ducked into the office supply room to collect my list of items. I wanted to make sure the office was fully stocked before I left. The door was just shutting behind me when I heard it open back up. I turned with a smile to greet whoever had joined me when I saw it was Peter. My face froze.

"What are you doing?" I demanded.

"Why, I'm getting supplies Cass, I just need a few things over here...." and he quickly reached around me as though going for the shelf and instead grabbed me around the waist, pulling me close.

"I know what you really want, and I'm going to give it to you." He had both arms wrapped around me grasping my hands behind my back and was trying to kiss me on the lips, putting in a pretty good effort to force his tongue into my mouth. I was squirming and telling him to quit, but every time I opened my mouth, he shoved his tongue inside. I was just thinking about whether or not I had enough room inside the small closet to knee him in the nuts when suddenly the door swung open and in walked a man I had not seen in the offices before. I managed to yelp,

"Stop it! Get away from me!" He quickly let go and turned to face the stranger that had walked in. As soon as his face turned the stranger took a quick and effective punch at Peter's face and then walked out. Peter turned back to me and spat,

"Slut! This is your fault, you stupid bitch!" and then he walked out of the supply closet holding his face and letting the door swing shut behind him. I stood there breathing heavily for a few minutes trying to calm myself and gather my thoughts.

"What a total asshole" I muttered quietly under my breath. "Men like that deserve to be shot. And I'd like to be the one to do it." I opened the door a crack and looked out. Since I didn't see Peter anywhere, I boldly walked out and sauntered down the hallway to my office. Margaret looked up inquisitively again and asked me once again if everything was ok. Once again, I lied to her and told her I was just feeling emotional about leaving in two days. She smiled warmly and told me that everyone here would miss me as much as I was going to miss them. Yeah, it's true, I would miss them, but Peter was making leaving a whole lot easier.

Friday afternoon Margaret and the others in the office had planned a little surprise party for me to celebrate my last day. There were about 15 of us gathered in the main office space enjoying cake and coffee and having some laughs about funny stories we had shared during my time there. I was feeling a little sad to go, a little scared to start a new chapter, and a little excited about what may lay ahead. It was 3:00 pm and we were starting to wind down when the door crept open. I saw a hand around the door and a head poke in.

"Hey, I heard there was a party here". I was pleasantly surprised to see the man who had punched Peter on my behalf.

"Come in, come on in" one of my office mates invited.

"We are just saying goodbye to our very special "intern" Cassandra. She's moving on and we'll miss her very much". The man strode over to me and grabbed my hand firmly.

"So nice to meet you Cassandra, I'm...." and before I could hear his name the fire alarm went off in the building and suddenly everyone was grabbing their stuff and dashing for the door. I only had my coat and purse, so I grabbed it and ran down the corridor and outside with everyone else. By the time I got outside I couldn't see the handsome stranger anywhere. I caught sight of Margaret and thanked her for everything. We had hugs and a tearful goodbye and by then I had to run to catch my bus.

Chapter 44

A Real Job and a Real Life

I had put out so many resumes that I ended up getting four job interviews at various offices. Two of the positions were as a secretary, one was as a receptionist at a law firm, and one was as a personal assistant. I ended up being offered three of the positions and in the end chose the receptionist job at the law firm. It was an easy bus ride away, the pay was very good, and the people that interviewed me seemed really nice. They talked a lot about the culture and it kind of felt like a nice big family – and I could really use another place to plant some roots and get a sense of belonging.

The next few months kind of flew by with learning to answer the phone, manage the emails, and book appointments. It was a blur of fast-paced learning, meeting a lot of people, and beginning to find my place. I was coming up on 6 months at Cedar Crescent and had settled into a very comfortable way of life there. I began visiting my sister and her family every Sunday. When they started asking me to Sunday dinners, I couldn't have been more thrilled. My nieces were amazing, and they loved me so naturally and so purely, it made my heart burst when I walked through the door and the two of them shrieked and lunged at me, one sitting on my foot, arms wrapped around my leg, the other up in my arms stroking my hair and telling me how pretty I was. I was in love with these two little girls. And I really credited them for having put me on the right path. If I hadn't been so desperate to have a relationship with them, I may not have been so desperate to climb out after hitting rock bottom. I even went and visited my parents every now and then. Though it was mostly strained and awkward. They never really got over the things they learned that I had done, and I never really got over what I considered to be a shitty and abusive childhood.

Alex and I sometimes went shopping on Saturdays or had lunch downtown. She began suggesting it may be time for me to transition back to living on my own soon. I wasn't in any rush, so I usually told her that I'd think about it, then didn't. After another month of asking, she pressed me a little harder,

"Listen Cass, if you stay too long, you'll become too dependent and moving out on your own will become harder and harder. You've been clean for over eight months now. I think it's time. You need your space, you need to be independent, you need to prove to yourself that you can do this. And I really think you can. Don't you think it's time to go home?"

"No, to be honest, I really don't want to. I want to stay at Cedar Crescent forever. It's like being a teenager here – you never really have to grow all the way up" I grinned up at her sheepishly.

"Fine, I'll start working towards it," I relented.

"But first I want to save a little more money. And I don't want to leave before Sarah's birthday – that's coming up next month. And they really rely on me in the kitchen. I don't want to just bail on them...."

"Ok, ok, enough excuses already" Alex chuckled. I'll give you another two months. For the next two months I spent my Saturdays with Alex sprucing my apartment back up. We gave it a fresh coat of paint, a good cleaning, and replaced much of the décor with more cheerful artwork that suited my new perspective on life.

Work continued to fulfill me. I was meeting a lot of new

people and being invited to a lot of social events, which I mostly declined out of fear of being faced with drugs or alcohol and not knowing how to handle it. I hadn't so much as had a cigarette or drink of alcohol since entering rehab. Coffee was currently my worst offence. I also started going to the gym. I had joined a gym right by my office and took aerobics classes or worked out on the cardio machines at least three times a week. I was very much feeling in charge of my life. More than I ever had before in fact. I knew that I was ready to move back out on my own. And I knew I'd be fine. I had put so many structures in place for having a busy and fulfilling life, that I rarely even thought about the concept of getting high anymore.

The move-in went smoothly, although the goodbyes at the Cedar Crescent were tough. I cried a lot. And took forever to say all of my goodbyes. I kept making the girls promise to come and visit me, and I kept promising that I would come back to see all of them. Sarah had already moved out a few months back, and she was reportedly doing fine, which helped ease my anxiety. In my heart I did know I was going to be ok. And it was true - I really was going to be ok.

Chapter 45

Sometimes You Just Get Set Back

I was loving living back on my own. At first, I was a little out of sorts with the quiet and the alone time. I did my best to fill the quiet with TV, music, talking on the phone, and having visitors over. But I really was ready to grow back up and do life as an adult again. Only this time would be different. This time I would think before I acted, look before I leaped, and all that cliché stuff that apparently has a very real place in the grown-up world. I had passed the learning curve hump at work and could sail through my days with ease and competence.

It was around 10 am on a Friday when I looked up from my desk to greet a client of one of the lawyers and nearly choked on my coffee.

"Hello, miss, could you please tell Mr. Davis that I'm here, he's expecting me at 10 and I'm in kind of a rush. Thanks."

"Ye...yes...of course, just a...." I trailed off and leaped from my desk, shoving past him and racing for the staff washroom. I threw open the door and retched into the toilet, narrowly escaping bathing my shoes in chunks. The cold sweat prickled my forehead, and my head began to spin. It was him. It was the flabby rumpled man in khakis that had done me the service of ass-raping me in his car, and then leaving me for dead on the street side so I could get fifty bucks for my next fix.

I wanted to run. I looked for a window to escape through, but there was none. I cleaned up my puke and then stood for a few minutes, leaning against the wall, wishing I could run away. I felt so humiliated. I felt like the low life scum that he had treated me like. I suddenly felt so ashamed. I didn't deserve this job, this life, the nice friends I had. I was a fake, a phoney, a great pretender. I was getting up every day and pretending to be a successful grown-up woman who had her shit together. Instead, I was just a low life slut that probably had deserved to be choked to death that day.

After a few more minutes of sniffling and tearing up and swiping at my eyes while feeling sorry for myself I turned and looked in the mirror. Who was Cass even? Was I a high-priced dominatrix? Was I a low-life heroin addict? Was I a desperate street hooker? Or was I a receptionist at a nice law firm with nice friends and a good life? It started to dawn on me that I was none of these things. And I was all of these things. And I was actually whatever I said I was. It occurred to me that I was my inventor....so who did I want to be? Did I want to be a snivel-ling whiny victim stuck in the bathroom so I could avoid making eye contact with a disgusting abusive man? Did I want to let my past define me? Definitely not. So, who was Cass then? In that moment, standing in the staff washroom, staring at myself in the mirror with mascara smeared under my eyes, I decided who I was. I had gotten through so much in my life, and none of it had killed me yet. I was tough, I was a fighter, I was a survivor.

I hastily wiped off the smeared mascara, flung open the bathroom door, and practically pranced back to my desk. I sat down in my seat, raised my head up, and looked across the room boldly to make eye contact with the despicable man who had al-ready seated himself.

"Well, is Mr. Davis going to be seeing me soon? This waiting is unacceptable!" He snapped.

"Mr. Davis will see you when he is ready. In the meantime,

I suggest you sit yourself down and wait politely, or feel free to leave our offices immediately." And with that, I picked up the next call and promptly turned my back on the vile excuse for a man.

Chapter 46

Panic

Dave and I were shopping for new towels a few months after I moved in. We were having a hard time deciding between tan or cream and I told him he was being impossible. He retorted by flicking me playfully with a towel, but for some reason I wildly overreacted. I shrieked loud enough that the sales lady's eyes shot up as though she thought I was being stabbed.

"Sorry Babe, I was just joking around" he tried to explain, but for some reason this just made me angrier. I had been overly emotional lately, but sometimes that happened just before my period. He came and hugged me, and I cried, looking up at him ruefully. Then I burst into a big smile and began to giggle. I'm pretty sure Dave thought I was crazy. And I was - crazy for him that is. I was loving my new life so much. I was "adulting" like crazy and loving every minute of it. Except that lately I had been feeling a bit run down and had been taking a lot of naps. After actually fainting a few days later, at Dave's insistence, I went to see my doctor.

I waited in the waiting room for over an hour, during which time I went back and forth between boredom, annoyance, and panic. What if now that I finally had my life in order, I'm terribly sick with something. What if I have terminal cancer? What if I only have 6 months left to live? Oh my God, the thoughts just wouldn't stop. I was starting to believe the voices inside my head that told me I had to be punished for the years of immoral behaviour and just generally being a shitty human. I was terrified by the time I was called in to see Dr Rayburn. She was friendly enough and seemed very professional. She asked me a lot of questions, then sent me for a myriad of tests. When I got home Dave jokingly inquired "So, what are you dying of then?" I didn't think it was at all funny, so I burst into tears, then crawled into bed for a nap knowing I wouldn't get my test results for a few days.

Chapter 47

You Never Know Who You're Going to See

About a month after my run-in with my old john (who, incidentally, did not seem to recognize me at all), I was asked to supply snacks and coffee during a mid-point break in a lengthy meeting. I came in with my usual cheerful upbeat demeanour, and proceeded to skirt about putting out coffee urns, cups, cream and sugar, cookies, muffins etc. I was fussing with some of the items on the coffee table, when I heard from behind me "Excuse me miss". I turned around while holding two coffee cups, and I was so startled I almost dropped them. My mouth fell open. Our eyes met. Suddenly, his face relaxed into a warm and generous grin. "Well, hello Cassandra!"

Chapter 48

Results

A week later I was called back to Dr Rayburn's office. Once again, she kept me waiting in terrified suspense. She finally called me in. She began to look over her notes, clearing her throat every now and then, flipping pages, raising her eyebrows. She finally looked up and said, "Well, you seem pretty healthy Cassandra. You have no diseases or infections, your blood pressure is good, your nutrition levels are good…. although I would recommend you adding folic acid supplements." With that she just stared at me for a few seconds. "Ok, is that everything"? "No, there's one more thing" she continued. I leaned in; eyebrows raised.

Chapter 49

Dave

I couldn't believe who I was seeing. "Wow, hi" I stammered. Dammit, I never caught his name. I turned back and slowly put down the cups, and then turned back to him. He reached out his hand to me. "Hi, I'm Dave".

Chapter 50

Surprise

"Y ou're pregnant".

Chapter 51

How it All Comes Together

I spent the rest of my year working, living alone in my apartment, and fostering healthy friendships that felt supportive. Sometimes I met up with girls from the halfway house, sometimes I gathered with friends from work. I often saw Alex, who had also completely transformed her life. She was now in a serious relationship and working towards her real estate license. I was now comfortable drinking socially without fearing I would have the urge to use, as alcohol had never been my issue. I managed to keep off cigarettes, and knew I would never, ever go back to drugs.

As a way of getting complete with my past, I had started working on a biographical short novel about my life. It was at times extremely cathartic, and at times heart breaking to relive my story. But it helped me let go of my past and experience being grateful for what I now had. I was grateful for sobriety; I was grateful for my sister and my nieces. I was grateful for all of the cooking lessons Martha had given me. I was grateful for Alex and the other close friendships I had made along the way. I was pretty much just grateful to be alive.

Mostly, I was grateful to have run into Dave again. After the meeting, he stopped by my desk and asked me how I was doing. We chatted for a while, and then he left. I noticed that I felt flushed and had the feeling of butterflies in my stomach. What was this, a crush?? Whatever it was, it was new, and it felt amazing. I knew I wasn't yet ready to start dating, but it felt really nice to be interested.

Since Dave and some of the lawyers from my firm were working on a big project, I would often see him at our office for meetings that year. Sometimes their meetings would last for hours, and I had the pleasure serving them coffee and snacks on their breaks. I tried to be cool about it, but I still managed to blush every time he smiled at me.

Eventually he asked me out. It was innocent, he just asked me to go for a drink with him after work.
"No, I can't" I snapped, walking away immediately. He asked me a few more times, and I always muttered a very bad excuses and walked away. Eventually, he stopped asking. It would be approximately another year before I ran into him again, and I told myself it was for the best.

The day he strode into the office it took me by surprise. I found myself blurting out,
　　"Hi Dave, so nice to see you again, how've you been, here let me take your coat" I blathered on like a ridiculous schoolgirl. He politely replied and then moved quickly into the boardroom. Damn! I hadn't meant to be rude to him in the past, I had just panicked as I knew that I hadn't been ready to consider dating yet. But lately I had been feeling the urge to start dating again, albeit slowly.

I realized I would have to take matters into my own hands. I had to do something to figure out how to get him to ask me out again. I honestly had no experience with this, no game whatsoever. As he was leaving, I ran and got his coat.
　　"I have your coat, you should come for a drink with me, hi, I mean, have a good night. Ok bye". It was the worst bit of rambling that could have come out of my mouth and I was horrified.
　　"Sorry, um, ok, goodnight" I sputtered. He turned, looked at

me with a slow grin spreading across his face.

"Yes, yes I would love to take you out for a drink".

"I'm not much of a drinker" I said replied shyly.

"How about coffee then?" he returned.

"Yes, I drink coffee. I mean, I'll drink coffee with you". He chuckled and took my number. Three days later we had our first date.

Chapter 52

The End is Not the End

We began very slowly. A coffee, a lunch, a trip to the museum. I was beginning to feel confident that I could one day I could even fall in love and have a healthy relationship. But some days, the past just came back a little to haunt me.

I knew I had to hurry; Dave was meeting me at the coffee shop in 15 minutes. I didn't want to fuck this up. I had distracted myself laying on my bed entertaining thoughts of what it would be like to have Dave bound and gagged and at my mercy. It was an addictive thought pattern, even though I knew it would never, and could never, happen. Dave just wasn't up for that sort of thing. And I liked to think I no longer was either. I noticed I had been caressing myself and allowing my fingertips to linger over my erect nipples and throbbing clit. I was not doing myself any favours showing up to meet him all wet and bothered. I slowly drew up my panties, pulled my shirt back in place, and forced myself out of my reverie and off of the bed.

Chapter 53

The End

After finding out I was pregnant, I decided it was a good time to finish the novel I had been working on, chronicling my past. It was a cathartic experience, one that let me fully and completely let go of my past before bringing my child into this world. This story is for her.

Dear Unborn Daughter, this is my true story.

I wouldn't say I'm nostalgic about my past. It's not that. It's more like bound. When I lay back and close my eyes, I can smell the leather, taste the adrenaline, feel the excitement, the thrill of the conquest. Don't get me wrong, I'm glad I'm no longer living the lifestyle, it's just that it seems to have a certain hold over me.

I grew up having to be somewhat of a pleaser. It was how I learned to deal with the trouble of being a kid in my house. There was an endless supply of drinking, yelling, and general abuse doled out by my father, and my mother thought it would be helpful if she criticized pretty much everything about my older sister and myself. I suppose it was her way of coping. We were a "good Christian family", and for them, that meant no matter what hell occurred inside my house, we were always sure to put on a happy face for the rest of the world. In the end, my own way of coping was to learn to be adaptable, always know how to fake it, and, most importantly, trust nobody. I not only took those qualities on, but I wore them like a badge of honour.

Even when I think back to my first boyfriend as a teen, it was nothing more than awkward attempt to be accepted; a feeble effort to make myself think I was good enough. I easily mistook his advances to mean that I held some sort of worth. In the end, the relationships never went far, I learned very little, and I certainly never succeeded in actually becoming close to anyone.

That is, until I met your father. This is my story. It's not pretty, but it's real.